STORM'S
EDGE

STORM'S EDGE

TONY HEALEY

A HARPER AND LANE MYSTERY

THOMAS & MERCER

Text copyright © 2017 Tony Healey
All rights reserved.

Published by Thomas & Mercer, Seattle

www.apub.com

Amazon, the Amazon logo, and Thomas & Mercer are trademarks of Amazon.com, Inc., or its affiliates.

ISBN-13: 9781612185316
ISBN-10: 1612185312

Cover design by Cyanotype Book Architects

Printed in the United States of America

For my girls:
Leah, Freya, Olivia, and Lola

1

Ruby waits under the shelter of an old tree, its branches stripped bare by the cold weather.

Lester walks toward her through the tall grass that juts from the freshly fallen snow like a sea of black hair on a white scalp.

"Lester."

He smiles. To everyone else, it is a freakish expression on his tortured face—but Ruby has always found it endearing. She's always seen the man beneath the monster.

He pulls something out of his back pocket. A tangle of white cloth. He hands it to her. "Wanted to fhow you fomethin'," Lester says, his deformed lips pronouncing every s with a lisp.

Ruby unfolds it. It's a mask of some kind—two rough eyeholes cut into the fabric. She looks up at him, frowning. "Lester . . . I don't know what this is."

She hands it back over. Lester removes the belt from his jeans, puts the hood over his head. Ruby backs up, unsure. The mask he has created for himself doesn't take shape until he buckles the belt around his neck, tucking in the white material.

Ruby gasps. "Lester, take that off."

"Thif if me, Ruby."

She continues to back away from him, knowing this meeting was a mistake. She should never have agreed to it. Should've listened to her gut and said no. "Please, Lester. You're scaring me."

He advances toward her, his eyes burning from the darkness cast by the holes in the fabric.

Ruby tries to run. Lester clasps his hands around her neck, pulls her down to the ground. He pins her to the spot, his breath escaping the white cloth in puffs of frozen vapor.

Ruby sobs, screams, tries to tear his arms away and free herself, but Lester is too strong.

"Why, Lester?" she asks, hysterical. "Why are you doing this?"

Lester looks down at her. "Because you're my princeff . . ."

Ida gasps for air, sitting bolt upright in the bed, soaked through with sweat, clutching the sheets. She tries to regain her composure, to resist the anguish tearing holes in her soul. In the darkness of her room, she draws the damp sheets up over her body, the shivers settling in.

Ida closes her eyes, and she is back there, at the house. Lester lying facedown in a pool of his own blood. Every second fresh in her mind, as if it just happened. Ida ignoring Detective Harper's calls for her to stay where she is. Getting down on the floor next to Lester. Placing her hands on his body. Making the connection. Watching him as a young man, befriending her mother—then betraying that friendship as he strangled Ruby to death.

Seeing everything that came after—the girls he killed because he saw Ruby in them. Reenacting that fateful day up at Wisher's Pond over and over and over again.

Witnessing Lester's fall toward oblivion. She thought the dreams of her mother's murder would stop now that Lester was dead. Now that his soul had been consumed by the darkness . . .

If only that were so.

She gets up. Goes to the bathroom. Fills the sink with hot water. She cups her hands under the water and douses her face. The mirror over the sink is steamed up, even with the door open.

Ida wipes away at it with her forearm, and there, standing behind her own reflection, is Lester—white hood over his head, belt tight around his neck, dark eye sockets cut haphazardly into the white cotton.

She shrieks, spins around, but she is alone. Turning back to the mirror, she sees only her reflection. A frightened woman, plagued by dreams. By memories that aren't hers.

Ida watches the mirror mist back over, as if from some invisible breath. She turns the light off, returns to bed. After a long while listening to the sounds of the house at night, she sleeps the sleep of the dead.

Chalmer is a small hamlet with a population of less than a thousand people. Ten miles southwest of Hope's Peak, it's a quiet place as featureless as the endless, flat farmlands around it. Rose's Groceries & Supplies is the closest Chalmer gets to a Buy N Save, but it serves its purpose well.

Ida grabs a basket and carries it through the entrance. As grocery stores go, it's pretty large—taking up three storefronts, its big white facade (with **Rose's** accented in bright pink) dominating the lower half of Main Street.

Ida doesn't like heading into town, but if she really has to, she goes early in the morning. There are fewer people, less hassle . . . and parking isn't such a bitch.

She walks up and down the aisles, filling the basket. In the baking section, she gets everything she needs to make cookies. She woke that morning with the idea in her head that she would whip up a batch. Sometimes, there is only one salve for the soul, and that is good old-fashioned home cooking.

Her grandmammy made her cookies when she was a little girl. When she and her mother would visit—though those visits were sometimes few and far between, depending on how well Ruby Lane was getting along with her father at the time—the old house would be filled with the smell of freshly baked cookies. Later, with her mother gone, Ida's grandmammy would bake regularly to cheer her up. And even after that, at the mental hospital, her grandmammy would make regular visits.

Without fail, there were enough cookies to last for days.

Ida swings by the alcohol department, deposits a six-pack of beer into her basket, and heads to the front of the store to check out.

The smell and taste of her grandmammy's cookie recipe is one thing she can count on to lift her spirits. Even if the memories connected with them are bittersweet.

There are two cash registers, manned by women in aprons. The old man in line in front of her glances back casually, his eyes going wide when he sees who is behind him. Ida ignores him. Since the Lester Simmons case, she has seen her picture in the local rag on more than one occasion. Some notoriety has come with it. The old man pats the woman in front of him, whispers something to her, and she, too, looks back at Ida. The woman tuts and shakes her head.

Ida's face goes hot. Suddenly the store feels too small, the walls pushing in on all sides. Sunlight hitting the front windows, turning the inside of the store into a sauna. It takes an eternity for the couple to check out, and as they leave, they both glance back at her again.

Ida puts her basket next to the register and avoids the cashier's gaze. She pays and hurriedly leaves with her bags. Outside, she sucks in a big lungful of air, her chest getting tight.

It's a panic attack. Give yourself a minute.

She heads for her truck, her heart skipping. She unlocks the passenger's-side door, sets two of the paper bags in the footwell, and then spills the contents of the third onto the seat. She scrunches the neck of the bag in her hand and leans into the cab, breathing in and out with the bag. Her pulse slows, steadies, until she feels like she can get a full breath at last. She takes the paper bag away from her face, repacks her groceries, and backs up a step from the truck. Her behind hits something, and she turns to see that she's knocked into Hank Partman, the owner of Past Times, a store farther up Main Street. Ida frequents his store on a regular basis to buy vinyl.

"Oh God, sorry!" Ida says.

Partman smiles with those ridiculously large, perfectly straight false teeth of his. "No worries. I was actually walking over here to see if you were okay."

"You were?"

Partman points toward his store. "I was outside and saw you breathing into the bag. Figured you might need help."

"No, it was just asthma. Don't worry about it," she says, trying to downplay the incident.

Partman shakes his head. "Ida, you've been coming to my store since you were a teen. I know you well enough to know that you smoke like a chimney stack. You don't have asthma. You were having a panic attack, weren't you?"

"Yes," Ida says stubbornly.

"But it's passed now?"

She shrugs. Attempts a smile that doesn't feel right—let alone look convincing. "I'm a bit of an expert."

"I can imagine," he says. "Look, why don't you come over to the store. I can make coffee. I've got new vinyl in. Don't rush off."

"No. I appreciate it, Mr. Partman," Ida says, walking around the truck to the driver's side, "but I must get going."

"Okay," he says. "Well, the offer is there."

"I know it is, and I am so thankful, but right now I think I've had enough of being gawked at." She throws her head in the direction of three middle-aged women on the other side of Main Street, talking in whispers and observing their exchange.

Partman watches as she starts the engine, pulls the seat belt over her. She winds the window down. "I'm sorry."

"Maybe next time," Partman says.

"For sure." Ida pushes the truck into gear and drives along Main Street. She takes a left onto Nareesh Avenue and heads past a row of businesses: a photographic-supply store, a florist, the real estate agent she's been working with to get her grandparents' house on the market.

Now she's faced with the prospect of returning home, where she has covered every reflective surface in the house, even though she knows it won't stop the haunting, any more than disconnecting the phone stopped it from ringing . . .

For years, she believed that if she confronted her mother Ruby's murderer—if she knew *why*—it would put her demons to rest. But now she knows that's not the case. What she saw in Lester Simmons's memories just before his life ebbed away was the terrible truth that he hadn't acted alone. That his evil had seeped into the bedrock of Hope's Peak and, even now, was still bearing fruit.

Her mother's murderer may be dead. But to truly avenge her, Ida knows that she must slash and burn until the poison that has taken root in Hope's Peak is gone.

Forever . . .

2

Van Morrison pours from the stereo on the kitchen counter. Frank Morelli loads the dirty dishes and cutlery into the dishwasher.

"Look who's suddenly domesticated," his wife, Marie, says, unimpressed.

Morelli throws a tablet of detergent in the machine and shuts the door, setting it to wash. "I'm going for a walk, have a smoke."

"When are you going to quit?" Marie asks him.

Morelli shrugs his jacket on. The temperature has dipped suddenly. "Quitting what? Walking?"

"No," she says, giving him a hard look. "You know what I mean. You planned to quit last month."

"I know, and I will," Morelli says. He pecks her on the cheek. "Just as soon as I've finished the pack."

"Heard that one before," Marie says with a roll of her eyes.

Morelli moves past her and opens the front door. Lotty tries to leave with him, and Morelli ushers her back inside. "No, girl, not this time. Daddy needs his moment of Zen."

"How long are you going to be?"

"I'm just having a smoke, Marie. I'm not running off with anyone."

"Just remember. I've got you to myself for the evening. I want to make the most of it."

Morelli winks at her and then shuts the door.

It's the dead of night. It's a good area—their combined salaries have made sure of that. Everyone keeps to themselves. It's a nice, peaceful neighborhood.

Morelli heads out onto the darkened street and lights a cigarette, coughing after taking the first draw on it.

Damn things are gonna kill me.

He watched his mother die from lung cancer, back when he was young. It took a long time for her to fade away—coughing up black poison, wasting away until there was nothing left of her.

He crosses the street. The houses are arranged in a huge rectangle around a communal park. Usually he'd take Lotty with him on these walks, but not tonight. He just wants a moment to himself. Morelli stuffs his hands in his jacket pockets and follows the footpath around the pond.

He would like to blame his inability to quit smoking on the stress he is facing, but in actuality he's never felt more at peace. When you reach the very center of a cyclone, you find yourself surrendering to a great, soothing calm. And if anyone is at the center of a shit storm about to break wide open, it's Captain Frank Morelli.

With Internal Affairs busily putting their case together, Morelli knows their full wrath will fall upon his shoulders any day now. But he feels peaceful about it. What comes out will come out. Will the whole affair end his career? Most definitely. When this is over, will he be able to finally live with himself?

Possibly.

Morelli looks up at the dark sky; oily tendrils of black clouds drift across the face of the moon.

He returns his gaze to the path ahead.

A man stands in the shadows of the overhanging trees where the streetlights do not penetrate, his features hard to make out in the dark.

Morelli's hand falls to the absent sidearm on his hip—the gun he hasn't worn for a long time, that he wishes he bothered to bring on these late-night walks of his . . . leaving it behind, he realizes, might have been a grave error. The man walks out from the shadows.

Morelli relaxes. "Jesus, Bill . . . what the hell are you doing here?"

Bill Marshall holds up a hand. "Evening, Frank. I remembered you saying this is where you take your walks," Marshall tells him. "We need to talk."

Morelli looks him over. The man is retired from the PD—he was a veteran when Morelli was still a detective—but he is mostly unchanged. Fatter, perhaps. "Let's sit, then."

They walk to one of the benches arranged around the pond. Morelli sits at one end, and Marshall perches on the other. Marshall lifts a silver hip flask to his mouth, takes a sip, then offers the flask to Morelli. "Care for some?"

"No, I'd better not," Morelli says. "What's this about, Bill?"

"This is a heads-up, Frank. I'm gonna talk to Internal Affairs. Fess up."

Morelli is taken aback. "To what?"

Marshall chuckles. "I like that you think of me as a good cop. Incorruptible. But I got my hands dirty years ago. Hid things that, maybe, should've never been hidden."

Morelli thinks about the files in the station's basement—the files he gave to Jane Harper and Stu Raley. The PD's dirty secret that led to his detectives stopping the serial killer Lester Simmons. Morelli pulls out a cigarette, lights it without offering Marshall one from the pack.

"I never knew you were involved," Morelli says. "Look, we all turned a blind eye now and then, but that's just how it was. I assumed that's *all* it was. Maybe that was my cowardice. Those women paid for it. Only right I should, too, for my part in what took place."

Marshall shakes his head. Looks at his flask before taking another sip of liquor. The moon slides out from behind the clouds, shining over the still surface of the pond. "Remember when we used to go fishing, Frank? Just the two of us?"

"I remember the time you nearly got your ass hauled over the side by that catfish. Remember that?"

Marshall laughs, though there is only the slightest hint of humor in it. Almost like he's going through the motions. "Took two of us to haul that sucker onto the deck. Still got the picture somewhere. Biggest I've ever hooked."

"Shame we put it back."

"Fish like that deserves to see out its days in the mud, you know? Didn't feel right to end it there on the boat."

Morelli shakes his head. "Always were a sentimental bastard, Bill."

"Look—" Marshall sighs, changing tack. "What we did. I ain't proud of it, Frank. But it was for the town's own good."

Morelli scoffs, the memories of happier times tainted by recent events, leaving a sour taste in his mouth. "You keep telling yourselves that."

"Did you ever look at those files in the basement, Frank? All those years, Claymore kept 'em going, off the record. Tracking the killer's methods. Documenting the *real* evidence. We had no idea—*I* had no idea—who the killer was. If we'd known, we would have stopped him. But if we couldn't stop him, what was the point of terrorizing the town? Until we could catch the bastard and stick a bullet in his head . . . we had Hope's Peak to think about."

Morelli looks at him. "When those dead girls started showing up again . . . The murders had to stop, Bill. One way or the other."

"You did what you felt was right. Well, me, too." Marshall stands up, stuffs the flask into his jacket pocket.

Morelli turns on the bench to look at him. "Why did you come here, Bill? Whatever you tell IA, it isn't going to dissuade them from scapegoating me."

"This is a nice neighborhood, Frank," Marshall says. "You made a good life for yourself."

"Bill?"

Marshall's face is grave. "I'm done living in somebody's pocket. When they learn what I'm about to do, they will come for me. That's why I wanted to see you tonight. Make my confession."

Morelli stands up. "What are you saying?"

"Just watch yourself," Marshall says. "You don't realize the lengths these people will go to in order to protect their own interests in Hope's Peak. Right now, all of us, everything . . . It's all on the table."

Marshall walks away and is soon swallowed by the shadows. Morelli calls after him, but he's gone. He pitches his cigarette butt out onto the dark water and walks toward his house.

Bill Marshall looked like the guts had been kicked out of him. Was that how he'd feel when IA was done?

Morelli fumbles another smoke out of the pack and slips it into his mouth with trembling hands. Goes to light it—but doesn't. Snaps his lighter closed, picks the cigarette from his lips, and looks at it. He suddenly has no taste for it. Feels sick to his stomach. He drops the pack of cigarettes to the asphalt and crushes it with his shoe.

He doesn't notice a car pulling up behind him until it's too late. He turns, hearing the soft oomph before he feels it.

Morelli looks down at his chest, his hand going to the patch of deep red blossoming beneath his jacket. The next shot tears through his neck, and he ends up on his back on the lawn—arms and legs useless, heart slowing, breathing coming in ragged, shallow bursts. Everything cold and getting colder.

The sky overhead is suddenly very clear, and Morelli thinks: *Marie will be waiting for me to walk back through that door. She wants me all to herself. Now she'll never have me again.*

3

"Tell me again. What's your profession?"

Jane Harper watches the doctor move the Doppler through the gel covering her stomach. Three months in, and she doesn't look pregnant, but the image on the screen says otherwise. Just twelve weeks since Ida told her she was carrying Stu's baby, and Harper can't believe what she's seeing. A head. Arms. Legs. The makings of a little person.

A graphic over the baby's heart shows the flow of hot and cool blood in red and blue.

Harper realizes the old man is looking at her, expecting an answer to a question she didn't hear. "Sorry? I was miles away."

"It's quite alright. I get it a lot. I was just asking what you do for a living."

Harper can't take her eyes off the screen. "I'm a cop."

"Ah. Right," Dr. Kandy says with a knowing smile. He zooms in on the profile of the baby's face. "Well, you and your baby appear to be in good health. Nothing out of the ordinary, I'm happy to say."

It's a moment she should have shared with someone, but she didn't think to ask anyone to come with her. No one in her life even knows she's pregnant yet. Apart from Ida, of course. In her head, she imagined the checkup being a quick affair, completely routine. But there is *nothing* routine about seeing a tiny life growing in your uterus for the first time. She looks at the empty chair next to her, where Stu might have sat.

"Are you okay?" Dr. Kandy asks.

Harper looks at the doctor and smiles. "Yes."

"Well, I'll pull the curtain. Use that blue tissue there to wipe the gel off, then put your clothes back on," he tells her. "I'll get you some pictures."

Postcards from impending motherhood. Maybe I should've watched Teen Mom *a bit more.*

The doctor closes the curtain around the bed, and Harper makes quick work of wiping all the light-green gel off her stomach. She gets back into her pants and blouse, then pushes the curtain to one side. Dr. Kandy hands her a set of black-and-white screen captures from the scan, and Harper's struck by how light they are for something that means so much.

"Thank you," she manages to say, barely able to take her eyes off them.

"I want you to take care of yourself."

"Yes. I know."

Kandy regards her with knowledgeable eyes that seem big behind the thick lenses of his glasses. "Be mindful of your stomach. Of getting hit, or, uh . . ."

"Shot?"

"Yes. Getting shot wouldn't be advisable in your condition," Kandy tells her. "If you need me to write you a note, telling whoever is in charge that they need to treat you with kid gloves, I'm more than happy to do so."

Harper starts laughing.

Dr. Kandy looks at her with his head tilted to one side. "What's so funny?"

"Come on, Doc. Cut me a break. What do you think I'm going to do when I come up against an armed man, or a rapist? Whip out my note and ask them to play nice?"

"I just want you to be careful."

Harper rolls her eyes. "It doesn't work like that. Anyway, I'll be fine," she says and starts counting off on her fingers. "No kicking doors in, no T. J. Hooker rolls over the hoods of cars."

"And . . ." Dr. Kandy holds up a finger.

Harper smiles. "No getting shot."

"That's right." Dr. Kandy opens the door for her to leave. "Take care, and I'll see you in eight weeks. And remember to stay away from the caffeine. I'm afraid for the next six months, you're going to be decaf exclusive."

"Yes, Doctor. Of course. I wouldn't dream of doing otherwise."

There are worse places to be buried, I guess.

Harper climbs the steep slope of the cemetery, walking through the rows and rows of white headstones that jut from the lush green grass like giant teeth. The sky is a faded blue, with fat, round clouds on the horizon like the sails of distant ships. There is a chill to the breeze, the first bite of fall in Hope's Peak.

Despite everything that has happened, Harper never considered leaving town. It would seem wrong, somehow, to run from strife again. *Trouble finds me no matter where I am.*

Harper sights Stu's headstone. The flowers she left there the last time are gone—blown away on the wind, or cleared away by the groundskeeper.

"Hey," she says, arriving at the foot of his plot. She lays a fresh bouquet of flowers on the grave. From up here, she can see all of Hope's Peak: the distant ocean, the harbor, the sprawl of the town itself, the old wood mill to the left. It's a glorious view, and she knows Stu would have appreciated it.

"Nice day," Harper says, sitting on the grass and looking around. The watery sun makes the sea shimmer like mercury. "I like coming up here."

Harper looks at the headstone. **STUART RALEY** is embossed at the top, his date of birth on one side, the day he died on the other. A date she will never forget for as long as she lives. Harper reaches out, strokes the front of the stone. It's cool to the touch—as if she expected anything else.

"Good news today," she says, fishing the scanned pictures out of her bag. She can't stop looking at them. Now it seems real. Before, it was a case of taking Ida at her word. Then two over-the-counter tests, both of which were positive.

Her first scan, at eight weeks, showed the tiny beginnings of a baby. No more than a bean. But it had already fluttered with life. However, she hadn't felt the same tug of emotion as she had this morning. That promise of life from four weeks ago had grown and matured; it had the stubby beginnings of arms and legs, a face. A heart that beat strong and true.

"It's happened so fast. It feels real now. Before I was just kind of getting my head around it all," Harper says, as much to herself as Stu's grave. She takes one of the scans and tucks it beneath the flowers. Harper sighs. Touches the letters of Stu's name, her heart aching in her chest.

Once a week, religiously, she's made the pilgrimage to the cemetery to visit Stu. He had a hero's funeral, with most of the Hope's Peak PD turning out in full-dress uniform for the service. His ex-wife, Karen, attended, a black veil failing to hide the mascara streaking down her face. Karen had been a crazy bitch in the past—going so far as to come to the station and remove a handful of Harper's hair. They'd had their differences, sure, but at the funeral Harper surprised herself by throwing her arms around Karen and holding her tight. They'd both lost something in common—a man they loved. Even Morelli looked cut up as Stu's casket was lowered into the chasm that would be his final resting place. Something in his expression—in the shadows under his eyes—hit Harper where it hurt.

Still did.

As for herself, she got through the day, coasting on a numb cloud of shock, until later that evening, alone in her apartment. She lay on her bed, staring up at the ceiling, hand on her stomach. Ceiling fan pushing the warm air around and around. She imagined the pyrotechnics, in miniature, playing out inside her—the spark of life that would cling to her, rely on her, and grow within her. Stu lived on in the life she now carried, and that thought was overwhelming sometimes.

What will I do?

How will I raise this child alone?

She has no doubt her former partner, and lover, would have made a phenomenal father to their child. It's frightening enough bringing a baby into the world. But to do so on your own feels like a special kind of punishment.

As she looks down over Hope's Peak, the light shifts as the clouds cross the face of the sun, and Harper is hit with the same deep sense of loss that has driven her to come here so often. She knows there is nothing really here, just his body below the ground, his headstone bright white under the sun, the flowers she brings. What is tangible is the baby inside her. The part of him that lives on. Coming here reminds her of that fact.

Harper stands, regarding Stu's grave. "I really didn't think it'd turn out this way," she says.

At that moment, a gust of wind rushes up out of nowhere, as if in answer.

◆ ◆ ◆

The Hope and Ruin Coffee Bar is packed.

Dr. Kandy's words of warning ringing in her ears, Harper orders her grande latte to go. She grabs a tall iced tea for Ida and then heads to her car. Clipping in her seat belt, Harper is conscious of the way it stretches across her stomach. It doesn't hurt, and it isn't uncomfortable, but her hand goes there anyway. It's hard to ignore now.

She slips into the flow of traffic heading out of Hope's Peak and takes sips from her coffee as she heads for Chalmer. Fields fan out on either side of her as she leaves town behind. Bon Jovi spills from the radio when she switches it on, and at first it's jarring, but she leaves it. She's always regarded Bon Jovi as lesser kin to the E Street Band, but she can't deny how catchy many of the tracks actually are. The fields are different now: the main crops harvested, some of the ground turned over for rotation, and hardy winter crops taking their place. In the distance, crows take flight from an advancing red tractor, their black shapes rising awkwardly into the milk-white sky.

Stu wasn't even in the ground before Internal Affairs dove in on what happened with Lester Simmons, seizing her report and any evidence that had been collected up to that point and throwing their whole case under extreme scrutiny. Their investigation was twofold: the historical cover-up of the murders that took place in Hope's Peak and the concern of the investigators over Ida Lane's involvement . . .

From the outset, the media were all over the Simmons case—particularly Stu's untimely death. While almost everyone she knew in Hope's Peak was in attendance at Stu's funeral, an underground videographer calling himself Cypher gained access to Lester Simmons's house and uploaded footage to YouTube. The video was listed as *Hope's Peak Killer House of Horrors* and went viral within hours. It showed the hall, the stairs, the hole in the plaster from where Lester smashed through it—as if the house were some chamber of secrets worthy of the public's fascination.

Regardless of what the local rags wrote about the case, offering their ill-informed opinion on every aspect of it, Harper knows she did what was right.

She drives through Chalmer, the radio shifting gears from a steady run of rock and roll to Patsy Cline. She sips her coffee and almost hates herself for not following Dr. Kandy's advice and ditching the caffeine.

Great start to motherhood.

4

Caution tape snaps in the breeze, stretched across the front of Captain Frank Morelli's house. The man himself is on his back, a plastic sheet covering him. Albie has already seen Morelli's face, frozen in confusion, eyes fixed on some far-off place.

The whole street swarms with uniforms. One of their own has been taken out.

"There you are," a gruff voice says from behind him. A heavy hand falls on his shoulder. Detective Gerry Ramirez is in his early sixties, with a thick gray moustache and salt-and-pepper hair thinning at the top. A persistent aroma of cigars follows him everywhere. For all Albie knows, it could be the man's natural scent. He took six months off for a knee replacement and missed the drama that befell the Hope's Peak PD. The man now walks with a noticeable limp. Pairing him with younger, more physically fit Albert Goode was one of Captain Morelli's better decisions—for both their sakes.

Albie has learned a lot from the older, seasoned cop.

Ramirez squats down next to Morelli's body, knees popping from the effort. He peels the plastic sheeting back. The neighbors are watching from their lawns and top-floor windows.

"I can't believe we're here," Albie says, feeling his cool slipping.

Ramirez points to the bullet holes. "Nobody reported hearing gunshots. I'd wager whoever shot him was using a silencer, which means a professional."

"Makes sense," Albie says.

"This was close range," Ramirez tells him, turning at the sound of an approaching vehicle. He nods his head in its direction. "An execution."

"I think we've got company," Albie says. He watches the unmarked car roll up, wheels bumping onto the curb. Engine still running, a woman exits the passenger's side dressed in a dark-navy-blue suit and matching heels. She's middle-aged, with short blond hair, her face drawn and deeply lined, and the worn appearance of someone who lives on caffeine alone.

She snaps on latex gloves as she walks toward the caution tape and ducks beneath it. "Who's running the scene?"

Ramirez raises a hand. "That'd be me."

"You are?"

"Ramirez."

She offers one gloved hand. "Lizzy Freehan. I'll be acting captain for the time being. I was appointed this morning by your mayor."

Surprise registers on Ramirez's face. "Right."

"And you are?" Freehan asks Albie.

"Albert Goode."

Freehan nods, then turns to the cadaver at their feet. She casts her eyes over Morelli's body. "Forensics?"

"Ten minutes out," Ramirez says. "They've been held up."

"Unacceptable," Freehan snaps, covering Captain Morelli's body. "I want this man off this lawn ASAP. I don't want him out here for all to see."

"Understood."

"The family is inside, I take it?"

"Yes, ma'am," Ramirez says.

She pulls her gloves off and hands them to him before turning to Albie. "Detective, you're with me," she says, heading for the house.

Albie hurries after her, glancing back to see Ramirez looking confusedly at the gloves in his hand—as if Freehan has handed him a used prophylactic.

◆　◆　◆

The place never looks any different, Harper thinks as she pulls up next to Ida's red truck. *It could still do with a good lick of paint.*

She has visited Ida several times since Lester Simmons was caught and killed, but not as frequently as she would like. Whenever she calls to arrange something, Ida never answers. Today she drove here on a whim, hoping that Ida would be in.

Harper checks her cell phone. It's dead.

Damn. Forgot to charge it last night. She opens the glove box and finds the power bank she purchased a few weeks before. Charging directly from the car battery makes her nervous; a hang-up from her teens, when she'd driven secondhand cars because that was what she could afford. Blasting the stereo without the engine running would leave her with a dead battery.

Harper sets the power bank on the passenger seat, connects the phone to it, and leaves it there to do its thing. She grabs the iced tea from the holder and gets out of the car.

Ida appears on the front porch. "Thought I heard someone drive up here."

Harper walks up the steps and hands Ida the iced tea. Most of the ice has melted, but it's still cold, the cup perspiring in her hand.

Ida sips the drink and smiles.

"I remember you said it was the best you'd ever tasted," Harper says.

"That I did. Come on, sugar, let's sit down." Ida leads her to the swinging chair around the side. Harper remembers her first visit here, thinking the bolts holding it in place looked too rusted, too old to take anyone's weight. But when Harper sits in it, the fixings don't budge.

Ida sets the iced tea on the boards, stands with her back against the porch railing, and pulls a cigarette from a pack. "Mind if I smoke?"

Harper shrugs. "Not so long as you stay over there."

"Fair enough," she says, lighting it. "I appreciate you coming out here. It's a nice surprise."

"My pleasure. It'd be easier if you answered your phone once in a while," Harper says, frowning. "I mean, it'd be even easier if you lived closer to town, but—"

"Well, that might happen soon."

"Huh?"

"I've put this place up for sale."

Harper sits forward. "Really? Why?"

Ida shrugs. "Time for a change, maybe. I've spent so damn long out here, living like a hermit. I can't explain it. I feel like . . ."

"Dipping your toes in the water?"

Ida grins. "Yeah."

"Well, I'm surprised, I really am," Harper says. "And pleased, of course."

Ida's life has not been the same since her involvement in the Lester Simmons case. Before she had been living on the edge of society, in her grandparents' place, existing in the long shadow cast by her mother's murder. Now, when Harper looks at her, Ida is different somehow—a newfound confidence showing itself. In the way she moves, in the way she stands.

Ida looks at the fields stretching out under the pale sun, at the distant line of trees, stark against the washed-out horizon. She has the wistful look of someone who has languished for far too long.

"It's been a long time comin', I guess," Ida says.

"You'll do fine."

"I was thinking of moving to Hope's Peak. Get out of Chalmer and start over."

"Wow. You've really given this serious thought, haven't you?" Harper asks.

Ida blows smoke from the side of her mouth. "It's not just that I'm getting restless . . . there's something else."

"Go on."

"There's been some misery here, and this house has sucked it up like a sponge. Don't get me wrong, I've never felt like I shouldn't live here. Not at all. It's always been home. But every now and then, a taste of what's in these old walls comes through. Sometimes the wind kicks up out here, and even though I know it's just the eaves sighing, I can't help but feel like that sound's coming from the house itself."

"Three months ago I would've said you were crazy," Harper admitted.

Ida draws on the cigarette, releasing the smoke through her nostrils. "You're one of the few people I can talk to about this, Jane. I keep thinking about the move *you* made, coming to Hope's Peak from San Francisco," she says. "Bet that was daunting."

"It was a bit," Harper admits. "But kind of nice at the same time. Knowing that I would be a stranger. It's what I needed."

Since their experience with Lester Simmons, Harper has wondered how Ida is coping. To have a gift like hers is not normal and to experience what she has is even worse. Reading the dead the way she does *has* to take a toll.

Ida pitches the cigarette away half-finished. Sits next to Harper on the swinging chair, reaches across, her warm hand on Harper's wrist. As their skin touches, Harper feels the connection—two frayed copper wires brushing up against one another, a charge running through the both of them.

Harper doesn't have to look up from where Ida's hand rests on her wrist to know that her eyes are closed. To know that she is sifting through the maelstrom of jumbled, confused emotions Harper has swirling inside. To know that Ida is wading through that thick soup of imperceptible feelings like an explorer in some wet, swampy jungle.

"Ida . . ." Harper begins to say, not wanting the connection, not wanting to share with Ida what she is feeling. But she hears a voice in her head.

Everything vibrates.

Harper swallows. She can taste the latte from her drive over. She closes her eyes, realizing that the bond between them is running both directions. There is darkness, and a telephone ringing. Not just that—raw emotion, too. Rising up from deep down inside. Ida is doing a good job of concealing it, but now Harper feels it.

Anger.

The telephone gets louder and louder and louder until Harper is forced to open her eyes.

Ida is back at the railing, holding the plastic cup of iced tea, taking little sips.

Harper looks down at her wrist where Ida's hand had been, the feeling of symbiosis fading, the current that ran between them receding, getting weaker and weaker until it sputters out altogether.

"What was that?" Harper asks her. "Don't you think you should, like, ask my permission before doing that?"

"Sorry."

Harper cocks an eyebrow. "What did you find?"

"A lot of confusion," Ida tells her. "A lot of fear."

Harper looks at her, frowning. "I heard a telephone ringing when we were connected."

Ida pales.

"It got louder and louder," Harper continues. "So loud I had to open my eyes. It was too much. What was all that about? Does it make sense to you?"

"No," Ida says, face tight.

Harper cocks her head to one side. "You don't sound convincing."

Ida stiffens. "It means nothing. Trust me."

"Okay," Harper says. "There was something else, too. A feeling."

"Go on," Ida says.

"I felt anger," Harper says, frowning. "Really intense anger."

Ida looks away. Swallows. "Everybody got something to take care of, sugar. Just the way life is. You got yours . . . I got mine."

"Ida . . ."

She looks back. "Honestly, don't you worry none."

Harper checks the time. Sighs. "Look, I'd better go. I'm a bit dead on my feet, if I'm honest."

Ida looks at her—*really* looks at her—and says, "You still think about him, from time to time, don't you?"

"Who?" Harper frowns back at her.

"You know *who*, Jane. That awful man in San Francisco. I've seen him attacking you. He's never far from you and is the root of your fear."

Harper rubs her throat. She swears that sometimes she can still feel his hands there, pressing down harder and harder. Choking the air out of her. Whatever Ida has seen, she's not wrong in determining that the serial killer they called The Moth back in San Francisco left a permanent emotional scar. Most detectives have only one or two really memorable cases that define their careers.

I've had my quota already, Harper thinks, wondering how much of that time her friend saw. "I guess that case has been on my mind lately."

"Why?"

"The symmetry, I guess. Lester Simmons cost me my partner. The man you saw—the papers called him 'The Moth.' That whole case cost me my marriage. My life, really. I came here and started over."

"Can't blame yourself, sugar."

Harper smiles softly. "Ida, do you think it's possible to move on from the past?"

"Not sure. What I *do* know is, you can't escape it. That much is for sure. Always has a way of catching up with you in the end."

Harper climbs into her car.

"Thanks for coming out here. And thanks for the iced tea."

"Anytime," Harper says. She slips on her shades. It's not sunny, but it's still bright. Living in Hope's Peak, you get used to wearing your sunglasses in all weathers, simply out of habit. "When do you think you'll sell?"

"Soon. I've got a guy coming around here. He's going to take pictures, take measurements, or whatever the hell it is these real estate agents actually do."

Harper laughs. "Yeah, it's one of those mystery professions, isn't it? A lot of money for very little work."

"Sounds to me like it's the right job to be in."

"Please think about letting me help you find someone to talk to. It's only a few phone calls, on my part, and I can set it up. It's honestly no bother."

"Last thing I need is more shrinks, Jane." She looks back to the house. "I'll get by."

"If you change your mind . . . ," Harper says dubiously.

Ida turns back. "Would *you* take it?"

"It *was* offered to me actually."

"And?"

Harper starts the engine. Clips her seat belt in. She looks at Ida with a wry smile. "See you later."

Ida steps back. "Just what I thought."

5

It never gets old. The soft hiss from the speakers, the drop of the needle, falling into the groove. The imperfections of the vinyl's oily black surface. Ida closes her eyes, Bob Dylan's voice lifted by the confident bass on "Sweetheart Like You."

For a moment—as always—Ida is carried away. As a matter of preference, she's found Dylan's earlier efforts to be stronger. But he did some good stuff later on, too. *Infidels* gets regular play in her house. Something about its soft reggae vibe and the emotion coming through the lyrics keeps drawing her back. She sways on the spot, lost in the guitar riffs at the close of the song.

The telephone rings, and the moment is lost. Ida opens her eyes. Her throat constricts, tightens, loses all moisture.

Is there no end to the torture?

Jane got too close to the truth when she visited. Shortly after what happened at the Simmons house, Ida's phone rang incessantly. At first Ida had ignored it. Thought that it was maybe the press looking for an exclusive. A spin on what had taken place.

But after days of listening to the phone ring, she finally picked it up.

Lester was there.

She knew the voice that spoke on the other end as surely as she knew her own. It was distant and scratchy but undeniably *his*. *"Ruby . . . if that you?"*

Ida slammed the receiver into the cradle, but moments later the phone rang again.

Trembling all over, Ida lifted the receiver, pressed it to her ear, and listened. Static on the line—like waves falling on a shore—and then the sound of breathing. Faint. Barely audible.

"Princeff . . ."

"Leave me alone!" she screamed. Right into the receiver, emptying her lungs, spittle flying from her mouth, heart pounding behind her ears. She violently hung up the phone, wiped her mouth, and backed away.

I know that it's not really ringing, she'd told herself, suddenly cold all over. *I know it's something leftover from my connection with Lester. Some kind of residual evil at play.*

But this morning the phone started ringing again. Ida didn't answer it this time, just yanked the cable out of the wall. Lifting the phone off the table, she nearly jumped out of her skin when it rang in her hands, vibrating with the sound. She ran through the house to the back, threw it into the tall, dry grass, and slammed the door shut behind her.

Now it is ringing again. With no connection. With no power. By no earthly means. She knows it's in her head, which makes it worse.

And Jane wonders why I don't want to talk to a professional . . .

Ida turns the stereo up, the whole house trembling from the volume of the music. But not even Bob Dylan can drown out the telephone. It's there. Ringing and ringing. Lester letting her know that, despite death embracing him in its velvet arms, he's sticking around—wants to talk. Ida tries to block out the noise, but it remains at the periphery.

Ringringring.

"Enough of this shit," Ida says, charging into the kitchen and to the cupboard under the sink where she keeps her little tool bag. She unzips it, riffles through the screwdrivers, spanners, loose screws, and wire scraps to the heavy, rubber-handled hammer at the bottom. It feels good in her hand. Weighty. Solid.

Bob Dylan blasts from the stereo as she throws the back door wide open. The phone, old and heavy, sits in the middle of a depression in the long grass. It is shaking. Ringing and shaking. Ida lifts the hammer with both hands and, teeth clenched tight from effort, brings it down on the phone. Up, above her head, swinging it down in an arc again and again. Something takes over her, a primal need to destroy the thing. To end the mental torment once and for all. She smashes the telephone until it falls to pieces.

Until it rings no more.

Walking back inside, panting from the effort, Ida craves a cigarette. When Jane visited, Ida worried that telling her friend the truth would result in another long-term stay at a psychiatric hospital that she knows she would not survive. She wonders what Jane would make of the scene that just transpired in the backyard. Her pulverizing an old telephone with a hammer like someone possessed. Like a madwoman.

I'd be put away for sure, she thinks, setting the hammer down on the kitchen sideboard and taking a cigarette from the pack on the windowsill. Ida lights it, takes a long draw, holds it, then blows the smoke out through her nostrils.

She feels lighter. There's a sense of relief that comes with knowing the telephone will never ring again. But she knows all too well that the phone itself was never the issue. It's what's got inside her head—what's left of Lester Simmons—that's the problem.

That's something the hammer will not fix.

6

Freehan had gotten the call that morning: the mayor's office was specifically requesting her as interim captain due to Captain Morelli's absence.

Well, absence *is a bit misleading,* Freehan thinks as she watches Morelli's widow tell her story again. Opening the door when he didn't return from his walk. Finding him on the lawn.

Mayor Crenna made short work of bringing her up to speed on the quagmire the Hope's Peak PD had found itself in. But, of course, she already knew most of it. There had been a serial killer on the loose for decades. Accusations of a cover-up—supported by files hidden away, chronicling the murders in grisly detail.

"Internal Affairs are having a field day," Crenna said. *"Can't say I blame 'em."*

"I can imagine. It's quite a scandal," Freehan replied.

Crenna grimaced. Looked out the window of his office. *"Press is in their element, obviously. Every day there's another column about it. An opinion piece. I'm getting sick of it."*

The press was a pain in the ass. Always had been. *"I saw the video that was leaked, from inside the house,"* Freehan said, shaking her head. *"Gets like a feeding frenzy, doesn't it?"*

"Vultures will snatch at any juicy morsel they can find," Crenna said, turning around to face her. *"Morelli didn't know how to handle the press. But I saw how you handled that case in Jacksonville. That was smart. That was what I call proper leadership."*

"Thank you."

"Take control here, Lizzy. Handle this. I need your experience."

"From what I can see, the Hope's Peak PD already has a scandal, Mayor. It doesn't need another one," Freehan said.

Marie Morelli buries her face in her hands. "I can't answer any more questions," she sobs.

"I understand," Freehan says, motioning to a female cop to move in and comfort her. "I want to assure you that I will not rest until your husband's murderer is found."

She turns to Albie and whispers, "Outside."

Morelli's body is being loaded into the back of the coroner's van. Where he lay, the grass is covered in sticky, jammy blood.

"Everything under control, Detective?"

"Yeah," Ramirez says. "CSU just removed the bullets, and they're taking them to the lab for testing."

"Good. Keep me posted."

Ramirez strokes his moustache as he watches Freehan duck under the caution tape and stride back toward her car. "What the hell was all that about?" he asks.

Albie shrugs. "Wanted to break the news to Morelli's wife herself. Told her she was in charge now and that she'd do her best to find the shooter."

Ramirez shakes his head. "Shit's gonna hit the fan when the press gets wind of it."

"Yeah?"

Ramirez cocks one eyebrow. "You think that whole affair with Harper and Raley was a big deal? Wait till the press finds out the police captain has been assassinated on his own doorstep."

Mike McNeil, the medical examiner, slams the back doors of the coroner's van and walks around to the driver's side. His assistant, Kara, crosses the lawn, removing her rubber gloves.

"Detectives," she says.

"Hey, Kara," Albie says.

She looks at the blood on the grass and swallows. "We're taking the captain in now. Give us a couple of hours, and we'll have the preliminary results of his autopsy for you."

"Thank you," Albie tells her, then watches her leave.

Ramirez shakes his head. "What's a sweet kid like that doing workin' in a morgue?"

"Weren't *you* a sweet kid once?" Albie asks.

"Never."

Albie walks toward his car. "I think I believe you."

He tries Harper's cell to give her the bad news about Morelli. She should know. Captain Morelli took her on when she wanted to get as far away from San Francisco as possible. He supported her and helped her settle in. Harper should be here, working the crime scene with them.

No answer.

Damn it, Harper. Today of all days.

The white sun bulges on the horizon when Harper pulls into the parking lot of the Buy N Save. She pushes a cart inside the store and makes quick work of getting everything she needs. In this regard, she follows

Dr. Kandy's orders—plenty of fresh fruit and vegetables, oily fish, and dairy. She allows herself one pack of cookies for her sanity—there are worse vices.

Harper pushes the cart to the bakery department, looking for a whole-grain loaf of some kind. Toasted with butter and jam. She's not sure that Dr. Kandy would approve of the butter, but jam has to be one of her five a day, right?

A blonde has her back to Harper, reading the label on a pack of cinnamon rolls. *Looks familiar,* Harper thinks. *Where do I know her from?*

As the woman turns around, Harper sees that it is Stu's ex-wife. Their eyes meet, and Karen says, "Oh," clearly taken by surprise.

Harper lifts a hand in greeting. "Hey."

"Didn't know you shopped here," Karen says stiffly.

"I never used to," Harper says. "Dinner used to consist of takeout and *reheated* takeout. But I've been trying to eat healthier."

Karen nods, eyes falling on the cookies in the cart.

"Well," Harper says with a shrug. "I didn't say I was a saint."

Karen smiles genuinely enough. "In all fairness, you did say you were *trying.*"

"How have you been?"

Karen shrugs. "I keep going. Things have to move on, don't they?"

"They sure do."

An uncomfortable silence falls between them, both of them reaching for something else to say and coming up empty. "Well . . . ," Karen says.

"I'd better go. It was nice seeing you again," Harper tells her.

Karen puts the cinnamon rolls back on the shelf. Either she didn't really want them or she's just lost her appetite. "Nice seeing you, too," Karen says, moving away.

Harper wonders if Karen suspects anything, and she feels suddenly self-conscious about the slight bump pressing against her shirt. Barely noticeable, except to her.

At least she never asked why *I'm trying to eat healthier. The last thing I need is to tell her that I'm pregnant with Stu's child. A child he tried to conceive with her until their marriage crumbled.*

She takes her things to the checkout, just wanting to get back to her apartment. After her short hike up to Stu's grave, and her drive to Chalmer and back, she's bushed. Already, the pregnancy is starting to impact her in ways she would've never imagined.

The groceries fill two bags. Harper carries them outside and crosses the parking lot to her car. As she juggles the groceries to get the keys from the bottom of her handbag, she spots a man on the sidewalk passing by the parking lot.

"Bill!" Harper calls, setting the bags on the ground. He looks around, but doesn't see her. She waves her arm in the air. "Bill, over here!"

Detective Bill Marshall retired the same year she joined Hope's Peak PD. He has a shock of gray hair swept back over his head and looks like an aging Elvis in his too-tight jeans and dark-blue shirt tucked beneath the overhang of his belly.

"Hey there!" he shouts, about to walk into the parking lot to come speak with her. "Hang on a second, I'll walk around."

"Okay."

A loud noise catches Harper's attention—a car screeching around the corner, tearing up the road. Marshall turns toward the sound, too. The car decelerates rapidly, drawing up next to him, the driver's-side window sliding down.

It suddenly dawns on Harper what is about to happen. She drops her groceries and holds out both hands, eyes wide. As if she can stop it with a gesture. "No!"

Marshall frowns back at her, confused, as the driver of the vehicle reaches out, arm fully extended, a pistol at the end of it.

Marshall's chest explodes outward.

One hole.

Another.

Bullets burning right through him, throwing up clouds of red mist. His eyes clamp shut, and Harper watches as he staggers forward against the railing separating the parking lot from the sidewalk. Clutches onto it as if he is sliding along the deck of a listing ship, blood gushing from the exit wounds.

Harper watches the driver level his gun at her. She ducks behind her car as he opens fire. One bullet thuds against the right wing. The back window blows out, shattered glass raining down. She clamps her eyes shut, covering her head with her hands.

Tires squeal on the asphalt as the car speeds off. Knowing she's in the clear to move, Harper gets up, runs through two rows of parked cars. Bill Marshall has collapsed completely, his top half strewn over the railing. Harper runs into the road, panting, and watches as the car careens left at an intersection and is gone, the sound of its engine fading into the distance.

She rushes back to Bill's side and eases him down off the railing.

"Bill!"

He looks up at her. Eyes so wide, so scared.

"It's okay," Harper says, looking around for someone, anyone. She holds his hand. "You're going to be alright."

His mouth is working. Trying to say something. Harper leans closer. Marshall's voice is barely a whisper.

"Sorry . . ."

His gaze clouds over. His body goes limp. She lowers him to the recovery position. He doesn't make a sound, and when she presses her fingertips against his neck, there is no pulse. Harper closes his eyes, takes a deep breath, then gets up.

A man in a suit is frozen to the spot, cell phone clamped against his ear, looking on in horror. Harper demands that he give the phone to her. He hands it over in shock.

She dials 911 and reports what has happened, but she doesn't hear her own voice—she's functioning at a base level, training and instinct kicking in, as if there's not enough CPU to handle anything else. You can be a cop and work the beat for years, but you never get used to being shot at. It still makes your hands shake to see a good man gunned down in front of you, the flame of life snuffed out in seconds. It's only after the fact that the reality of what has happened sinks in.

In the moment you are a product of discipline.

You have to be.

There is a steady gathering of people around Marshall. An old woman removes her jacket and drapes it over his body to give him some dignity. Harper looks down—the blood beneath his body is so dark, it's almost black.

Harper sits on the ground, hands instinctively going to her stomach, to the new life inside. She closes her eyes, drawing in deep breaths in an effort to fight the urge to vomit.

Not here in front of all these people.

The wail of approaching sirens grows louder and louder. Harper feels a hand on her shoulder. She looks up.

"Jesus," Karen says, face pale, eyes wide. "Is he dead?"

Harper nods, unable to say anything. Thoughts crawl through the avenues of her brain like molasses.

"Are you okay?" Karen asks. "I saw you getting shot at. I can't believe it."

Harper barely hears her. The gunshots ring and ring in her ears, like the telephone she heard when Ida touched her. Over and over and over.

7

"And you're pregnant?" the nurse asks her, eyebrows raised.

Harper sighs. "Like I told the other nurse, I've been checked over already today. I had my twelve-week scan. I'm fine."

The nurse removes the armband connected to the blood pressure monitor. "That was before you were *shot at*. We like to examine pregnant ladies who have been *shot at*."

"I can appreciate that," Harper tells her. "But I'm a key witness. I need to get out of here."

"This your first kid?" the nurse asks, unmoved.

"Does it show?"

"Kinda. What you've gotta get your head around is that you're gonna be pricked, prodded, and examined from now until the baby arrives. Get used to it. You get in a car accident? We wanna check you over. Bumped your head on the kitchen cupboard? We wanna check you over. Guess what? Got shot at today and nearly died? Well . . . big surprise, we wanna check you over."

"I see your point," Harper says sarcastically. "Thank you for enlightening me."

"Don't mention it." The nurse pats her hand. "I'll go update your file, then you're free to leave."

Is that for good behavior, warden?

The nurse leaves, and Harper is left with her own thoughts for company. She can still see Bill Marshall getting shot down. Dying in front of her. It's hard to shake, just like it's hard to rid her ears of the gunshots that have left them ringing.

She looks down at her stomach, at the beginnings of its bump. Her pregnancy will announce itself as her favorite tops and sweaters are relegated to the back of the wardrobe. She's chosen not to tell anybody yet because things at work are already complicated by the IA investigation. Throwing the issue of her pregnancy into the mix . . .

But I'll have to tell them eventually. When I start to show—in a way that can't be blamed on pie and ice cream—I'll have to come clean. But until I need to, this secret's just for me.

Albie Goode pushes through the privacy curtains around Harper's cubicle. "D'you realize I'm only twenty-six? You nearly gave me a heart attack."

"Sorry I inconvenienced you, Albie," Harper says, rolling down the sleeve of her blouse. "I mean, it *was* my choice, getting shot at."

Albie shakes his head. "I saw Bill Marshall. Poor guy."

"He was walking toward me, not a care in the world. Next thing I know . . ."

"But *you're* okay?"

"Oh yeah. Takes more than a few bullets to stop me," Harper says, not wanting to tell him that she will have difficulty sleeping tonight. That the shots are still ringing in her ears.

"I tried calling your cell this morning, but it was off."

"Shit, it's probably still charging on the passenger seat and they're holding my car as evidence." She rubs her forehead. "What is wrong with me?"

Albie looks at her. "Harper, I've got real bad news."

"Go on."

He takes a deep breath. "The captain was shot dead last night. His wife found him. She said he went out for a cigarette, and when he didn't come back she opened the door and found him on their lawn. Ramirez and me got to the scene this morning. We're putting it all together. Like I said, I tried calling to tell you, but I couldn't get through."

Harper's eyes bulge. "Christ," she says, numb.

Albie falls silent for a moment. "Hey, I guess you don't know the latest, either, do you?"

"Jesus, there's *more*?" Her head is swimming.

"A Lizzy Freehan has come in to cover the captain's position while we investigate."

"They sure don't waste any damn time," Harper says, shaking her head. "It doesn't make sense. First Morelli. Now Marshall. Both within twenty-four hours."

"Do you think you were a target, too?" Albie asks.

"No. I think the guy in the car threw a few my way because I was in the wrong place at the right time. It was a spur-of-the-moment thing, I'm sure of it. The same can't be said for our two colleagues . . . Was Marshall under investigation by IA? Who would want to kill Morelli and Bill Marshall?"

Harper feels the sadness well up inside, and she pushes it back down. Not now. *Later.* Her hand goes to her stomach. Albie doesn't notice. He is looking at the curtains, lost in his own thoughts.

"I need to get to the station and give my witness statement." She slaps his thigh. "Come on. We've got work to do."

Interview Room 3 is already in use. Harper hesitates at the door. There is a woman talking to Detectives Dempsey and Sinclair, two IA officers handling the allegations of corruption in the department. The woman is wearing a navy-blue suit and heels. She's in her fifties, has blond hair cut short and a weathered face.

Has to be Captain Freehan.

Harper knocks on the door, and the two IA officers wave her in.

As expected, the woman rises from her chair and introduces herself, shaking Harper's hand. "I'm Lizzy Freehan. I'm stepping in for Morelli."

"Nice to meet you. I wish it were under better circumstances," Harper says.

Neither Dempsey nor Sinclair move.

"Detective Harper here knows who we are," Sinclair tells Freehan. "We've spoken on several occasions."

"Always a pleasure," Harper says snarkily, sitting down.

Freehan tells her that she'll be sitting in while Harper gives her statement. "Then we'll talk," she says.

Never a good sign, Harper thinks.

"Okay. Take us through what happened, starting at the beginning," Dempsey instructs her.

Leaving out the reason for the doctor's appointment, Harper details her morning—her visit to Stu's graveside, buying coffee at the Hope and Ruin Coffee Bar, and visiting Ida at her grandparents' place outside Chalmer. She tells the two IA detectives how she went to the Buy N Save, bumped into Stu's ex-wife, Karen, then paid for her groceries.

"So you walked toward your car," Dempsey says.

Harper nods. "Yes. I was sort of struggling to get my keys out of my handbag. You know, carrying the groceries."

"Right," Sinclair says without looking up, writing his notes.

"That's when I saw Marshall—"

Dempsey clears his throat. "Detective William Marshall. Retired."

"Yes. That's right," Harper says. She goes on to tell them how it happened from that moment on—how the blood flew from Bill's chest in a fine mist. How he slumped against the railing, then slid down at an awkward angle. How she ducked down behind her car as the shooter fired in her direction, the glass from the rear window showering over her. Harper feels no shame in telling them that she feared for her life.

She tells them that he died in her arms, whispering *sorry* to her with awful finality.

"Christ," Sinclair says.

Dempsey asks her, "Anything you can remember about the shooter?"

"I didn't get a good look at him. He had . . . dark hair. Maybe," she explains. "Mostly I just saw the gun."

"What about the vehicle?" Dempsey asks.

"No plate."

Sinclair looks up. "You mean it didn't have one?"

"No, it was covered up. There was some kind of dark material over it," Harper says. "The vehicle itself was brown. A sedan."

"Got all that?" Dempsey asks his partner.

Sinclair closes his notebook. "Yeah. I got it."

"I think that's it for now," Dempsey says, reaching for the recorder. "Interview finished at nineteen hundred hours."

"Hey, I don't get it," Harper says.

Dempsey cocks an eyebrow. "Don't get what, Detective?"

"You guys, coming in here and taking a witness statement from me. A bit below your pay grade, isn't it?"

Dempsey folds his arms. Adopts a cocky stance. "Not when it might have a bearing on an ongoing investigation, Detective."

"What's that supposed to mean?"

"It means we're already examining your methods. We want to be sure your conduct is in line with what we expect from a detective of your experience."

Harper shakes her head. "You think I'm lying about what happened . . ."

"Not at all," Sinclair says, standing next to his partner. "We will assess whether or not you followed protocol. Whether or not you're telling the truth about running into Bill Marshall the way you say you did. If all that checks out, you've got nothing to worry about, have you?"

"I am telling the truth," Harper snaps. "About everything."

Dempsey smiles, one side of his mouth lifting in a sneer. "I hope so, Detective. For your sake."

"Uh, thank you, Detectives, I think that's enough of that," Freehan says, opening the door for them. "I'd like a moment with Detective Harper now, if you don't mind."

"Of course."

Both detectives clear the room, closing the door behind them.

Freehan sighs. "Dicks, aren't they?"

"You can say that again."

"How're you holding up?" Freehan asks.

"Faring better than Bill Marshall, that's for sure."

"Detective Goode brought you up to speed?" Freehan asks, taking Dempsey's seat opposite Harper.

Harper sighs. "He told me Captain Morelli was found dead this morning."

"I'm sorry, Detective. I know you've worked closely with the captain since your transfer from the Bay Area."

"You've done your homework."

Freehan shrugs. "I was briefed this morning by Mayor Crenna."

"What did he say?"

"That there has been a lot of corruption. A lot of wrongdoing. I've been brought in to see that anything like that is stamped out."

Harper shakes her head. "Things sure do change fast around here."

"They do when one of our own is taken out," Freehan says. "Something, I believe, you're intimately aware of."

"Your point?"

Freehan looks at her intently, her eyes taking Harper in. "I don't like trouble, Detective Harper," she says finally. "I'm afraid that, right now, *you* are trouble."

"Excuse me? My boss has been shot outside his home. On top of that, I saw a man gunned down today. Damn it, *I* was shot at, too. I don't need you coming in here and accusing me of whatever it is you're accusing me of."

"I'm simply stating a fact. Trouble seems to follow you around like a bad smell."

"Oh?" Harper says, unsure of where any of this is going. What she does know is that she wants to get out of the room, get some fresh air.

"I'm impressed by your work with Detective Raley. Stopping that killer was some feat. You're gutsy, Harper. Not afraid to follow a hunch, to follow your instincts. I like that."

"I'm sensing a 'but' coming here," Harper says.

Freehan's face is stern. "But what I don't like is my people going rogue."

"I'm the first to admit that using a psychic isn't exactly protocol."

"That's an understatement."

"But without Ida Lane's help, Lester Simmons would probably still be out there. Whether you believe in her abilities or not, they gave us the break we needed."

Freehan sits back, hands folded in front of her. "My beliefs have no bearing here. Internal Affairs is still reviewing your methods, and we'll have to wait on their judgment. In the meantime, the Lester Simmons case has brought this department into disrepute. I already have the stigma of corruption hanging over my head. Whether you were correct in what you did to stop that killer—it's not my job to say. But right now, anything you touch will be tainted by your involvement."

"So what are you saying?"

Freehan opens her arms, as if to say: *That's all there is.*

Harper puts it together. "I'm getting benched."

"I think, for all concerned, it would be best if you took leave until we determine what, if any, connection there is between these shootings, the Simmons case, and the scandal."

Harper shakes her head. "You can't be serious!"

"You're obviously a good cop, and I believe that, regardless of Ida Lane's involvement, your investigation with Stu Raley will hold up to scrutiny. It was unconventional, from what I've heard, but it obviously worked. Your reliance on Ida Lane, and the role her participation played in the circumstances that led to Raley's and Simmons's deaths—that raises a lot of questions, Detective. But that will come. Until then, I want you to lie low and let us get on with our jobs."

"You're making a big mistake—I can help. I want to find whoever shot Marshall and Morelli. I need to," Harper pleads.

"Sorry. My decision is made."

"I don't believe this," Harper says, getting up, snatching her bag off the chair next to her, and blustering through the door. She moves through the office, a storm front that the other detectives and officers are eager to avoid. Passing Stu Raley's old desk—still vacant—she feels a stab of grief through her heart. If he were still around, he'd have fought Freehan on her decision. But on her own . . . That desk is an awful reminder of the vacuum Stu left when he died. Not only in the office, but in his support and encouragement. They were good together, and Morelli understood that.

Harper rushes into the sunshine, gasping for air, her heart fluttering. She paces back and forth in the entrance, hands at the small of her back. It takes a moment for her to regain her composure.

Time is running out. When Freehan eventually lets me off the bench, I'll be showing. She'll either make me take leave or stick me at a desk. This pregnancy will stop me from investigating Morelli's murder, and before too long I'll be no use to anybody. I can't just sit on my ass. I have to do what I can . . . I owe Morelli that much.

Harper starts across the parking lot, then remembers she has no car. Luckily, she was allowed to retrieve her cell phone from the passenger seat of her car before it was impounded as evidence. Not wanting to head back inside and ask Albie for a lift, Harper slips on her sunglasses and heads for the nearest bus stop. She hasn't needed to use public transport since arriving in Hope's Peak. For a moment she could be forgiven for thinking she's back in San Francisco . . . but such a thought would be too much to bear.

At the last minute she has a change of heart. She looks up and down the street until she spots an approaching cab.

Harper waves it down and gets in.

"Where to, my friend?" the driver asks her.

Harper does her best to recall Captain Morelli's address from memory.

8

Mike McNeil pulls the sheet down to reveal Captain Frank Morelli. His skin is an unnatural shade of slate gray.

Freehan folds her arms. Glances at Albie. "Are you going to be alright, Detective? You look green around the gills."

"I'll be fine," he says, thinking, *I won't be throwing up in front of you, that's for sure.*

There's a Y incision across Morelli's torso. Mike speaks into a digital recorder as he gives them the rundown.

"Sounds obvious, but for the sake of the record I have to be clear. The captain was killed by a nine millimeter. One through the neck where it severed the major carotid artery on the right. It tore through the adventitia, and the media, tearing it apart."

"Jesus," Albie says, shaking his head. "Do you think it was quick for him?"

McNeil glances up at him before continuing. "He would have bled out in minutes. If the severed artery didn't kill him, the bullet he took to the chest would have. It was a clean shot, dead center. Punched through his chest bone, took a slight detour, and exited just under his left shoulder blade."

Mike runs them through the rest of the results so far, then covers Morelli back up.

"Thank you, Mister McNeil," Freehan says, leaving the room, Albie in tow.

Kara looks up from her clipboard and gives Albie a sympathetic wave.

"See you," he says, closing the door behind him. They walk along the corridor toward the entrance. "So whoever shot the captain knew how to handle a weapon."

"Clearly," Freehan says.

"At least we know that much."

Freehan stops. Points back down the end of the corridor to the room containing Morelli's body. "Captain Morelli was shot. The shooter—surprise, surprise—knew how to shoot a gun. And right now, as of this moment, we don't know dick."

"We know that Morelli's and Marshall's murders are linked—"

Freehan shakes her head. "No. I want them investigated separately, for now."

"Why?" Albie asks, frowning.

"We can't let the coincidence of these two deaths determine for us that they are linked in some way."

"But they obviously are!"

Freehan glares at him. Mouth tight. "Are they? Can you be sure about that?"

Albie doesn't have anything to say.

"You have evidence? Or just the coincidence that the murder weapons are the same caliber?"

"Understood," Albie says bitterly.

"I don't know how Morelli ran this place, but I'm afraid I have higher standards," Freehan says. "Not to talk ill of the dead."

Albie thinks: *Too late.*

Detective Ramirez looks at her with surprise. "Didn't think I'd see you at work, all things considered."

"I'm no use to anyone sitting at home." Harper ducks beneath the caution tape. "How's it going?"

"Forensics are still on-site, but they've done everything they can." Ramirez stands with his hands on his belt like a sheriff in some backwater western town. "I'm just maintaining the crime scene until Freehan says otherwise."

"Our new leader . . . ," Harper says, hearing the bitterness in her own voice. "What do you think of her?"

Ramirez shrugs. "She's not Frank."

Harper looks from Ramirez to the spot of lawn where Morelli was found shot dead. "No, she's not. No Albie?" Harper asks.

"At the morgue with Freehan," Ramirez says. "This, uh, isn't a courtesy call, is it?"

"Nope. I want to talk to Morelli's wife."

Ramirez frowns. "Freehan talked to her earlier. Then a couple of guys took statements."

"I have my own questions," Harper says.

"Uh-huh. I'll bet." Ramirez regards her with weary eyes. "Go on through."

Harper walks inside the house. It's a large but modest home, with warm colors and oak flooring throughout. Framed pictures hang from the walls. The captain's family. His wedding day. Certificates and awards that span the course of his career in the Hope's Peak Police Department.

There is a picture of the captain's wife, Marie, dressed in her nurse's uniform, holding a baby. The photo must have been given to her as a gift because below it, inside the frame, a little plastic plaque reads: COMMEMORATING YOUR 1,000TH DELIVERY!

The place has been a home. Has history. They have lived their lives here, and it is filled with their memories.

If for only a moment, Harper can't help but envy the Morellis.

Back in San Francisco, her own husband couldn't stand the danger she faced every day on the streets. When she refused to transfer to a safer posting, he divorced her.

The captain must have seen times like that. But he stayed married. They got through it. Why couldn't Alex and I make it through to the other side?

She's wondered about it often. A person can go mad determining who was at fault and what might have been.

Morelli made a life for himself and had a career at the same time. He found balance between the two, and somehow he and his wife made it work. No easy feat. The question of balance has reared its ugly head numerous times since Harper discovered she was pregnant.

How will I manage with a baby?

Will I still be able to do what I do?

She pauses in the hall. Looks at a black-and-white photo of Morelli with his arm around Marie. Both of them smiling.

Happy.

Harper finds Marie Morelli in the kitchen at the breakfast table. Late fifties, early sixties. Brown hair. Eyes red raw, face pale white. She's wearing a thick sweater and leggings and looks completely frozen through.

Cold from shock.

A Labrador has its head in her lap. Marie absently strokes it, her expression distant.

"Mrs. Morelli?"

She looks up. "Huh?" Marie asks, completely dazed.

"I'm Detective Jane Harper. I wanted to drop by here, give you my condolences."

Marie nods. "Frank said you were the one who caught that killer."

"My partner, Stu, and I," Harper says. "But your husband risked everything to share critical information with us. Without it, we would never have broken the case."

Marie indicates the wooden chair next to hers. "Have a seat if you like."

Harper sits. "Your husband always made me feel welcome at the department."

"You're not from here, are you? I remember him saying something about you transferring from someplace."

"San Francisco."

Marie nods, remembering. "That was it," she says, looking down at the dog. "He said you had a bit of a reputation, Detective Harper."

"He did?" Harper says, frowning.

Morelli's wife locks eyes with her. "He said you catch bad people."

"I try."

"Another detective was here. She said she was stepping in to cover Frank's position for the time being. Promised me she'd do everything to catch his killer."

"Captain Freehan."

"Are you assisting the investigation, Detective Harper?"

Harper hesitates as Marie hugs the dog. She has always been amazed by the ability of dogs to sense their owner's pain. "I need to ask a few questions," she says softly.

Marie wipes her eyes. "Ask away."

"Did Frank mention receiving any threats before his death? Any suspicious phone calls or letters, any sense that he was being followed?"

"No. Nothing like that."

Strike one.

"Did he talk to you about any of the department's cases?"

Marie shakes her head.

Strike two.

"Did Frank ever mention a retired detective by the name of Bill Marshall?"

"I know of him," Marie says. "I remember meeting him at Christmas parties."

"Did he ever bring him up in private?"

"No." She frowns. "Why? Is he connected in some way?"

Harper shakes her head. "Not at all," she says, reasoning that it's better to conceal the truth for now. Marie can't help her in finding the connective tissue between the two deaths, and telling her that Marshall was also shot will only cause further distress.

"Well, I won't keep you any longer," she says, rising. "After the day you've had, I bet you just want some time by yourself."

Marie reaches out, grabs her wrist. "Wait. There was one case he kept talking about."

"Yes?"

"Yours."

Harper's mouth is dry. She has to clear her throat to speak. "Mine? The Moth?"

"The one we were talking about. The man who killed those girls," Marie says, letting go of Harper's wrist.

"And what did your husband have to say?"

"He said he had regrets. When I asked him what he meant, all he would tell me was that he wished something had been done sooner." Marie shrugs. "I guess there are some cases you never get over. That was one."

"I know the feeling," Harper says, her voice barely a whisper.

"When did you get in?"

"Two days ago, sir," Harper told him, taking a seat on the opposite side of his desk. "I found a place before leaving San Francisco."

"Oh?" Morelli asked, sitting down. "Whereabouts?"

"In town. Not far," Harper said. "Above a tackle shop."

"Ah, I see," Morelli said, smirking. "It's not what you're used to, I take it."

"No, but it's what I wanted."

Morelli looked down at some papers on his desk. "I've been doing some reading. That was quite a fiasco in San Francisco."

"It was, sir."

"But you got the bastard," Morelli said. "From what I've read here in these reports, this guy was a sick maniac."

Harper sighed. "Yes, sir. He was."

Morelli sifted through the papers. Searching for something. He seemed to find it. "There are fewer than a dozen murders a year here, with most of them solved in a week. We're not like the Bay Area, Detective. We don't have a lot of rapists, serial killers, or kidnappers here in Hope's Peak."

"That's why I came," Harper told him.

"Good," he said, peering at her. "So, are you looking forward to getting to work, Detective Harper?"

"Of course."

"Good. I want to introduce you to your new partner," Morelli said, pushing a button on his desk and speaking into it: "Raley, get in here."

A moment later a big man entered Morelli's office. Six feet, blond hair, muscular. "Sir?"

Harper rose from her chair. Shook his hand.

"Raley, this is your new partner, Jane Harper," Morelli told her.

"Nice to meet you," Harper said.

"Stu Raley," the man said. He released her from his grip. "Didn't realize I was gettin' a partner so soon."

Morelli raised his hands. "Well, here you are."

"I'm looking forward to working together," Harper told him. She meant it. A new place. A new partner. A new start.

Stu nodded. "Good. 'Cause we got a case already," he said, leading her out of the captain's office. "Last partner died on me."

"Oh. I see," Harper said, following him past rows of desks. "That's unfortunate."

"Fuckin' A," Stu said, glancing sideways at her. "You're not planning on dying on me anytime soon, are you?"

Harper considered. "Not this side of Christmas, no."
Stu grinned. "Know what? I think we'll do alright together, kiddo."

◆ ◆ ◆

The sun is sinking. Harper calls Albie and asks him to swing past, pick her up.

"Where are you?"

"Morelli's place."

"Are you joking, Harper?"

"Calm down, Albie. Just come pick me up."

"Jesus," he says, ending the call.

Ramirez is nowhere to be seen, though there are uniforms guarding the perimeter of the crime scene. Harper leaves the Morellis' front lawn and crosses the street. There is a park and a shaded area with trees surrounding a pond. She walks, trying to clear her head.

What a day.

The sky is burning with the colors of sunset. She finds a bench facing the pond and sits, craving a moment of peace and solitude. A momentary escape from everything.

Watching the water, she thinks about how much has changed since she came to Hope's Peak. Came running with her tail between her legs, looking for a new start. Broken by what had happened in San Francisco. Needing to find herself again.

A fish of some kind snatches a long-legged fly off the surface of the pond, dragging it down into the murky depths.

Harper determines that she will do all she can to discover the identity of the captain's killer, despite the fact she has been put on leave and ordered by Freehan to keep her distance from the case.

After all, being told not to do something has never stopped me before . . .

9

He crossed his parents' bedroom, the door ajar. Strange noises came from within, the sound of the bedsprings creaking. He looked through the opening and saw his father's bare ass pumping in and out, trousers by his ankles, white shirt gone see-through from sweat. His mother's legs at either side, the balls of her feet digging into the edge of the mattress. Both of them grunting, groaning, breathing heavily.

His friend from school was there, too. Billy Watkins moved him over an inch to get a look himself, his tongue to one side of his stupid mouth, and an even stupider grin on his face.

Billy's hand rubbed his groin through his jeans.

He pulled Billy to one side. "Come on," he told him. When they got outside, he asked Billy not to say anything to anyone, to keep it a secret.

Billy turned to him, still with the shitkicker grin. "Fuckin' her good though, ain't he? She must like the action," Billy said, laughing. "Surprised they ain't broke the bed!"

His fist smashed into Billy's face before he even knew what he was doing. It was a gut reaction. An instinct, deep inside, to somehow defend his mother's honor, for what it was worth. Billy's hands cupped his nose, blood spilling out between his fingers, droplets of it landing on the gravel drive at the front of their big old house.

"You busted my nose!" Billy mumbled, backing off. Without another word, Billy turned on his heels, running off down the drive, glancing back twice to make sure there was no chase.

He didn't run after him—just stood there in shock at what he'd done and watched Billy go, his heart beating fast. He'd never hit anyone before, and wasn't sure how he should feel.

What he discovered would change his life.

It felt fantastic.

It felt like power.

◆ ◆ ◆

Now, the boy is a man. "Damn cold in here," he says, stuffing his hands into his coat pockets.

The Waldo's Ice Cream and Refreshments factory in Chalmer is closed, all the workers given a half day and sent home. The cold storage at the back of the factory is the perfect meeting place.

The elders stand in a semicircle, dressed in heavy winter coats and gloves, a few of them stamping their feet to stave off the cold. There are fewer of them now—not that their influence has lessened as their numbers have diminished. He remembers creeping into that old house where they held their meetings when he was a boy. His own father among them.

The big fans on the other side of the cold storage blast them with subzero air. So noisy in there you have to shout to be heard. He is the only one whose face is bare, who doesn't bother to conceal his identity.

"We're disappointed," they say.

"You haven't been as proactive as you said you'd be."

He draws a breath, goes to speak, but is cut off.

"A public shooting?" one of them roars. "A ruckus the entire town is talking about!"

He clears his throat. "The guy I hired for that one went off the rails. Trust me, he's not a problem anymore. I dealt with him."

"Too little, too late," one of the elders snaps.

"Events are running you."

"We need this handled. Before we have to take action ourselves."

"I'm sorry." He sighs. Throat dry. "I'm going to fix this. Have I ever not come through?"

"You have our support."

"For now."

"Don't get complacent. Don't start thinking we're soft."

"Our patience is wearing thin."

The fans blow and blow. He can feel the elders' eyes pressing in on him. It's hard to tell who is speaking. They're all wearing the same white mask. Just a set of eyes in a smooth, blank face.

"I won't let you down," he tells them, and he means it. "I have things in place."

"We hope so," one of the old men says. He steps forward, distinguishing himself from the rest of the group. Points at him. "You're like a son to us. You know that. Your daddy was a good man. But don't get into the habit of thinking you're not replaceable. Everyone is."

He nods. Leaves the cold storage. When he glances back, they are still watching him from behind their masks.

Immovable.

Mysterious.

10

Mayor Hal Crenna stands behind a podium bearing the slogan **HONEST HAL**. There is a big microphone in front of his face. Cameras trained on him at all angles. His chestnut-and-silver hair is immaculately coiffed. Teeth gleaming.

"In the early hours of yesterday morning, Captain Frank Morelli of the Hope's Peak PD was found dead outside his home," Hal says, flashes going off around him. "The might of the entire department, headed by interim captain, Lizzy Freehan, is out in force. We will not rest until Morelli's murderer is found."

Some cheers. A few people clapping.

"This town has been tested these past months, but our resolve has never been stronger. We refuse to bow to acts of terror. We're better than that. You're *all* better than that," Hal says, looking at the reporters and press. "We *will* weather this storm. Thank you."

There are calls for questions, but Hal leaves the podium, making a quick exit. The gathered press is clamoring for more. For a headline.

The mayor of Hope's Peak leaves them in his wake.

◆ ◆ ◆

The morning rises over Hope's Peak. Harper leaves her apartment and walks to her car.

She catches movement on her right-hand side and turns around in time to see that it's a news crew. A cameraman and a reporter brandishing a microphone, followed by a boom mic operator and a man with a bright light on a rod.

"Fuck," Harper grunts, struggling to get her car keys out of her bag because she's in such a hurry.

"Detective? Can we have a few minutes of your time?"

Harper tries to hide her face. Keeps her head turned away from them as she tries her damnedest to find her keys in the bottomless pit of her bag.

"I'm sorry but no."

The reporter—a redhead in her thirties, dressed in a snappy suit with a little too much cleavage on display—thrusts the microphone near Harper's head.

"Do you mind?" Harper says, knocking the mic out of her way and inadvertently exposing herself to the camera in the process.

The reporter is undeterred. "What can you tell us about the murder of Captain Frank Morelli?"

"No comment."

"How about the ongoing investigation into corruption? I understand that Internal Affairs is now, as we speak, interviewing law officers in your department," the reporter says.

Harper glares at her. "No comment."

The woman hesitates with her next line of assault, then decides to go for it.

"What about your own personal dealings with a local recluse. Ida Lane? I have it on good authority you worked closely with her to catch Lester Simmons."

Harper steps forward. "Leave Ida out of this," she says, realizing, once she's spoken, what a mistake it is to have reacted to the prompt.

The reporter smiles thinly. "You like dismissing us, don't you, Detective? I guess it makes it easier for you, not having to answer for yourself."

"Sorry?" Harper rounds on her, the keys forgotten. "What did you say?"

The reporter has a sly smirk on her face. "Your involvement with a woman who spent years in a mental hospital. The death of your partner."

"You're out of order, and I'm not answering any more questions," Harper snaps.

"How about that last case you took on in San Francisco? What did they call him?" The reporter consults a folded sheet of paper in her hand. "The Moth? As I understand it, that last case ended your marriage . . ."

"Mind your own business," Harper says, her left hand plunging into her bag and, miraculously, landing on her car keys. She unlocks the car, then points at the cameraman. "And get that thing out of my face."

She climbs into the car and starts the engine. The reporter is looking at her through the glass. Harper stamps her foot down on the accelerator. When she looks in the rearview, they're still watching her.

Jon pours the tea from a small porcelain pot with a bamboo handle. He's roughly Albie's age, with short dreads and trimmed facial hair. He's thin, whereas Albie is thickset and muscular. The apartment they share in Hope's Peak is clean, tidy, modest. Exactly the kind of place Harper imagined Albie living.

Jon looks at her. "Sweet'N Low, Jane?"

Albie rolls his eyes, hands her the cup. "No, she takes hers as it is. She's sweet enough."

"That's not what you've told me," Jon says with a smile. "In fact, you said she was a bitch."

Harper looks at Albie, brows raised. "Oh, is that so?"

Albie walks to the living room, and Harper follows suit. "You'll have to forgive Jon. He knows not what he does. And he doesn't *think* when he speaks."

Jon sits next to Albie. "Pay no attention to Grumpy here."

"Well, it's nice to meet you." Harper lifts her cup. "And thanks for the tea."

"You're more than welcome. Albie's told me a lot about you."

"About what a bitch I am?"

Albie shakes his head. "No."

"Mostly," Jon says with a wink. He sips his tea. "He told me what happened to you yesterday at the station. You must be so pissed about getting pushed to the side like that."

Harper sighs. "Thing is, I understand why Freehan has to get me away from the investigation."

"Really?" Albie says, frowning. "'Cause *I* don't. You should be working the case with us."

"She doesn't want the Internal Affairs investigation interfering with this case. I get it. She's just doing her job. Doesn't mean I'm not angry about it, though."

"Sounds like your hands are well and truly tied," Jon says. "How long did you know the man?"

"Which one?"

Albie says, "I think he means Morelli. Jon, there were two deaths yesterday."

"Oh God, sorry."

"It's okay. I knew Morelli for as long as I've been in town. He really helped me settle in here, find my feet. I can't believe he's been taken from us like that."

Albie sits forward, holding his cup. She gets the feeling he's picking his words very carefully. "Harper . . . he was just as involved in covering up the deaths of those young women as all the others."

"You're wrong. He set me and Stu on the right path."

"Just how many are involved in this thing?" Jon asks, his voice lowered to a conspiratorial whisper.

"We don't really know," Harper says. "Internal Affairs is having a field day because this case has brought everyone's work into question. When Captain Freehan says that the whole department is tarnished, she's not wrong. At least, that's how it's perceived. Meanwhile, my methods are causing a whole lot of trouble for everybody." She drinks some of her tea.

Jon looks from Jane to Albie. "What have you got going on at that station, Albert? Your own little Guantanamo Bay?"

Harper laughs. "No!"

"Jesus, is that what you think we do there?" Albie asks him.

"No, I just—"

Albie shakes his head. "You think I'm there all day, attaching people's testicles to car batteries and getting them to confess to stuff they didn't even do? Come on."

His boyfriend gives him a stern look.

"It doesn't matter," Harper says, not wanting to get into it. She's had enough of explaining herself to the likes of the IA agents wanting to know the ins and outs of every decision, no matter how unimportant. "How did the autopsy go?"

"As expected, really. The captain took one to the chest, and the second bullet ripped an artery in his neck."

"Damn."

Albie sighs. "Mike said it was quick . . . which I guess is something."

"No witnesses have come forward?" Harper asks.

Albie shakes his head. "No. Several of the neighbors said that they often saw Morelli taking a walk. Smoking. Taking the dog over to the park."

"But none were looking out their windows the night he got killed," Harper says. "Typical."

"I've been thinking. What if he hadn't been out walking like normal? What if it'd been raining?"

"You're asking if the killer would've knocked on their front door, then killed the captain and his wife?"

"Yeah."

"I don't think so," Harper says. "Whoever killed him no doubt knew his routine, or they wouldn't have killed him where, and when, they did."

"True," Albie says. "So what prompts your visit, Harper? No offense, but you've never asked to come by my place before."

"I know," she says. "I feel really shitty putting you on the spot, to be honest."

His eyes widen. "Why am I worried about what's coming next?"

"Because it's asking a lot. It's putting you at risk, and I wouldn't ask if there was any other way around it."

Albie looks at Jon, who appears similarly concerned. He sets his cup on the coffee table.

"I need you to get me into the morgue," Harper says.

"Me?"

Jon looks confused. "I don't understand why you can't just walk in there yourself."

"Because I've been put on leave. But I want to keep working on this case. I owe it to the captain. Visiting his house yesterday, talking to his wife . . . I saw a side of him I've never seen before. The life he built outside of the department. Having a family, a marriage that lasted despite whatever he had to deal with during the day. That has to be honored."

"You sound different," Albie says.

Harper looks at him. "Maybe I am different. Lester Simmons . . . what happened at that house . . . Stu . . . it changed a lot."

Albie glances at Jon. "Makes you think about what's important."

Harper nods. "Look, there can't be any record of me going to that morgue. Freehan doesn't want me near the case, and with IA watching,

I don't want the rest of your findings questioned because I didn't follow procedure. Does that make any sense?"

"It does," Albie says.

"What do you want to go there for, anyway?" Jon asks.

"To see Morelli's body."

Jon makes a face, lost. "I don't understand."

"Freehan will implode if she catches wind that Harper's gone to the morgue. Especially if she does so with Ida Lane," Albie says. "I mean, I'm assuming that's your plan. That's why you want to see Morelli's body, isn't it?"

Harper looks at him. "Ida's the only way we can get a head start on this case. There's already been two cops killed. How many more are going to follow?"

"You definitely think this is the beginning of something, don't you?" Albie asks.

"I do."

"Even if you walk in with me, you have to sign in. Maybe Kara can help us," Albie says.

Harper frowns. "Think she will?"

"Worth a shot. I'm guessing we only need a couple of minutes."

"For what?" Jon asks.

"You wouldn't believe me if I told you."

11

Chalmer rests under a sky the color of dishwater. Harper cuts the engine and gets out of the car. Ida appears on the porch, wiping her hands on a dish towel. "Jane? I didn't expect you back out this way again so soon."

"Sorry to intrude," Harper says.

Ida steps down from the porch, her face grave. "What's wrong?"

"Captain Morelli was shot and killed outside his home."

"Jesus. Why?"

"I don't know. But that's not it. I watched another man—a retired detective named Bill Marshall—get shot down, too. Right in front of me."

"Damn, sugar. Are you okay?"

"Yeah. But I need your help. Your gift . . ."

Ida looks weary.

"I know it's a lot to ask."

A gust of wind blows dust and grit up off the road. "Jane, I don't know if I can."

"What's wrong?" Harper asks. "Are you feeling unwell?"

"Nothing like that. It's not a case of being unable," Ida explains. "More a case of being unwilling."

"Talk to me," Harper pleads.

Ida sits on her front steps. Pats the spot next to her. "What I did at that house . . . I've done it before. You know, been with folk when they passed, helped 'em along. Made it easier on 'em."

Harper sits down. "Okay."

"Some folks get mighty scared of what's coming, especially if they're sick. Probably why so many find religion when the end's near. Gives 'em comfort. But with Lester it was different. I've glimpsed the other side, the darkness, but there's a difference between seeing it from afar and being there when it happens."

Harper looks around. It's so still, so quiet, where Ida lives. Just the chirp of the crickets and the birds in the distant trees. Clouds washed out—pale-white milk dropped into a glass of water.

"What's happened, Ida? There's something you're not telling me," Harper says. "It's the telephone, isn't it? That's why you haven't been answering it."

Ida hangs her head. "I lied to you."

"I know, because I tried calling on my way out here, and it wouldn't even connect. It just rang and rang. It's like you've got rid of it."

"I have."

"Why?" Harper asks.

"Since what happened at the Simmons house, Lester's let me know he's still around, Jane."

"He's . . . *haunting* you?" Harper asks.

Ida looks at the ground. "I think so. Maybe not a haunting. Maybe it's something else."

"I think you need to talk to someone. Get everything off your chest," Harper tells her.

"I don't like shrinks, Jane," Ida says. "You know why."

"Look, I probably wouldn't like them either if I'd spent as much time around them as you. But these people are good listeners; it's what they're trained to do."

"What if they don't believe me? Or, worse, they recommend I go back inside?"

Harper pats the back of Ida's hand. "That won't happen."

"How can you know that?"

"Because I'd shoot them first."

Ida can't help but smile. "You're crazy."

"Says you."

"Okay." Ida looks at her. "If you really need my help, Jane, I'll do it. I've got this gift for a reason. I've come to realize that. And if there's a way of making whoever's responsible pay for what they've done . . . well, I'm all-in."

"Thank you," Harper says. She gets to her feet. Sniffs the air. "Is that cookies?"

"Yeah," Ida says. "They're probably ready, too. I can box us a few to eat on the road, if you like."

Harper follows Ida inside the house, mindful of the way the horizon has darkened since she arrived. "Maybe we can beat the weather."

The house is half-empty inside, the majority of Ida's belongings already packed away in anticipation of moving out of there. Ida leads the way to the kitchen, scooping up her oven gloves. The whole house smells wondrous. Ida glances over her shoulder. "Bad weather always has a way of catching up, sugar."

12

The boy threw the ball, and Roofy ran after it, tracking its progress as it arced through the air and landed at the end of the yard. He collected it in his mouth and ran back, tail wagging, dropping the ball at the boy's feet.

"Hey, Roofy. Good dog, good dog," the boy said, squatting down to pet the animal.

Harriet called him from the open patio doors. "Breakfast!"

"Coming," the boy called back, tossing the ball one more time, then walking inside. His mother and father were already at the table. His mother with her grapefruit and tea. Daddy drinking black coffee, with a half-finished plate of bacon and eggs in front of him. He sat reading the paper, uncommunicative as ever.

As the boy sat down, Harriet poured him a glass of milk. "Are you having your cereal today?"

The boy looked up. "Could I have toast?"

"Sure can."

"No, he can't," Daddy said, putting down the paper. "Boy's getting fat as it is."

The boy's mother didn't say anything. Her eyes were telling enough. Disgrace, disgust . . . and respect.

Harriet looked at Daddy.

He glared back at her. "You stupid, Harriet?"

"No, sir."

"Nothin' wrong with your fuckin' hearing, girl?"

She shook her head. "N-n-no, sir."

"Get to the kitchen, fetch my son his cereal."

"Yes, sir."

The boy looked down, ashamed. Roofy ran into the house, around the table, his tongue lolling out the side of his mouth.

"Get that fucking animal out of here!" Daddy roared, rolling the newspaper up and swiping at the dog as he circled the dining table.

The boy tried to intervene, but Roofy thought it was a game. Daddy tried to hit him with the rolled-up paper, and Roofy turned back, grabbing hold of it and yanking the newspaper out of his hand.

"HEY!" Daddy yelled, throwing himself back from the table and taking off after the dog.

The boy followed as Roofy ran outside, the paper hanging from his mouth.

"Get back here!" Daddy shouted. The dog stopped halfway across the yard. Looked back, panting. Tail wagging back and forth. "I said get back here!"

Slowly, cautiously, Roofy waddled back toward the house. To where Daddy stood, waiting for his paper. He stooped down to take it, but Roofy wouldn't let go. Daddy kicked out with his right leg.

Roofy backed off.

"Damn dog!" he snarled, snatching at the dog. Roofy dropped the newspaper and bit down hard on Daddy's hand. He recoiled, blood running down his wrist. Roofy ran off, barking.

The boy watched as his father stormed back into the house and headed for the back room, nostrils flaring, blood dripping over the carpet. His mother stood helplessly at the table, watching the scene, clutching her napkin.

Daddy returned to the breakfast room carrying his best golf club, clenched hard in his hand.

The boy got in his way. "Daddy, please—"

His father brushed him aside, sent him tumbling back into the table. Glasses toppled over, spilling juice and milk everywhere. He grabbed the boy by the front of his T-shirt. "Time you learned a lesson! This is your damn dog, so this is your fucking fault. That dog's goin' back where it came from. Should've known you weren't responsible enough to train it and take ownership!"

He paced off across the yard.

"No!" the boy screamed. Before he could chase after his father, his mom got in front of him, held him back.

"Quiet, son," she said in her soft, reassuring voice. He clutched his mother, burying his face in her side, squeezing his eyes shut as he sobbed and sobbed. "Daddy knows what's best . . ."

13

"You ready?" Harper asks.

Ida unbuckles herself. "Sure didn't think I'd be back here anytime soon."

"Not exactly the high point of my day, either," Harper says as she gets out of the car.

Albie crosses the parking lot toward them. "You both good?"

Ida looks at the drab mortuary. "Good as can be, I guess."

"Come on." Albie leads them to a side door at the east side of the building. A fire escape. Standing there holding it open is Kara, the medical examiner's assistant. She beckons them inside.

"Thanks for doing this, Kara," Harper tells her. "I really appreciate it. I know you're going out on a limb for us."

Kara nods. "Don't mention it. Albie's a friend, and when he said he needed a favor . . ."

"You won't get in trouble having this open, will you?" Albie asks.

"No more trouble than that time in college. D'you remember? With the dean's car?"

Albie fixes her with a serious look. "Kara, we're not back in college . . ."

"Stop worrying. I'll disable the alarm on it," Kara tells them, closing the door and turning a little key in the alarm panel next to it. "Our new guard never leaves the front desk, anyhow."

"Right," Harper says.

"Too busy stuffing his face with Cheetos, that one," Kara tells them. "What's all this about, anyway?"

Albie opens his mouth to speak, but Harper cuts in. "The captain's murder."

Kara holds her hands up. "Say no more. Well, I hope this helps you out."

"So do I," Harper says, glancing at Ida, standing nervously next to her. Quiet as a mouse.

"I'll leave you to it, but try not to be too long," Kara says, and then walks off down the corridor.

Harper and Ida follow Albie to a door at the very end of the hall, his shoes squeaking on the shiny linoleum.

"Albie?" Harper says.

He half turns to look at her. "Yeah?"

"What happened with the dean's car?"

"Not now, Harper," he says, walking to the door, putting his hand on the handle. Pausing. "You really want to know?"

Harper nods.

"We had this asshole dean. A complete homophobe. Used to walk to his car at exactly six fifteen, without fail. So one night me, Kara, and a few others, we tied a load of cans to the back of his car, and put a big sign over the rear license plate."

"What did the sign say?" Ida asks.

"It said, 'Just Married My Man.'"

Harper shakes her head. "Albert Goode, I never had you pegged as a social activist."

"I'd just come out to my folks, and they didn't take it too well. I guess the dean's bullshit just got me worked up," he says, ushering them into the room and then closing the door.

The chilled cabinets on either side of the room have metal doors that open out. Harper leaves Ida with Albie and finds the one labeled

MORELLI. The gurney slides out on its runners, Morelli's body covered with a sheet.

"Are you okay?" Harper asks Ida, her hand braced on the sheet. Ida nods but doesn't say anything. Harper pulls the cover back.

The captain's skin is ashen. His eyes are closed, face slack and relaxed, as if he's in a deep sleep. Harper wonders if his death was quick. Shot like that, she can't imagine him bleeding out over a long time and being aware of what was happening. If he was, there's no sign of it on his face.

The last time she was here, she and Morelli were watching the autopsy of a young woman. Lester Simmons's latest victim. Albie had to duck out because it got too much for him. She remembers Morelli's frustration—in his day, the sight of a dead body was a relatively common occurrence.

Harper reaches out, lays her hand against the icy clay of Morelli's cheek. "So sorry," she says, almost to herself. She feels an arm around her shoulder, and looks to see that it is Albie.

"Come on," he says, steering her away. "We don't have much time."

Her eyes swim with tears. "I thought I'd be able to hold it together."

They move to one side as Ida approaches Morelli's body. The air hums with static. Ida places one hand on Morelli's chest, just above where he has been cut open and stitched back together. Her other hand rests on his forehead. The lights flicker.

A moan rises from Ida's throat, long and mournful. She closes her eyes, and the lights dip.

Harper's mouth fills with a metallic taste, like copper, then her ears pop. She covers them with her hands. Turns to see Albie doing the same.

Ida's body shakes and jitters, as if she is being electrocuted. Albie starts forward, but Harper stops him in his tracks. He looks at her, confused and startled all at once.

Harper shakes her head. "Let her be."

The threads find one another. Fibers knitting together, forming an umbilical cord. There is tension, and resistance, as there always is.

Ida lets the joining happen.

The surf booms against the shore. Gulls circle overhead—white boomerangs cutting through the flat blue. A father and son cross the stretch of beach. Dad helps his boy wrangle a red kite as it dances on the wind.

Morelli unhooks the lead from Lotty's collar, sends the dog on her way. He watches as the dog runs to the edge of the water, hesitates when a heavy roller crashes, filling the air with cool white spray. Then she leaps into the receding waves with reckless abandon. Lotty comes bounding out of the water moments later—her big pink tongue lolling from her open mouth— running laps around him before rushing back in.

Ida hears Morelli's thoughts: I've never been happier.

Everything fades to shadow. Out of the black, there are stars, and a street—a quiet, leafy neighborhood. Oily tendrils of black clouds drift across the face of the moon in the sky overhead.

"I'm done living in somebody's pocket," Bill Marshall says, his face grave. "They'll come for me when they learn what I'm about to do. That's why I wanted to come here tonight and tell you."

Morelli stands up. "What are you saying?"

"Just watch yourself," Marshall says, walking away into the shadows. He turns back at the last second. "You don't realize the lengths these people will go to, to protect their own interests in Hope's Peak."

Morelli walks toward his front lawn. A car pulls up behind him. Morelli turns around. A man is positioned over the roof of a black Lincoln, his features obscured by shadow. He holds a gun. It catches the pale-white moonlight, flashing like a star in his hands.

There is a shot.

Morelli looks down at his chest, his hand going to the blossoming patch of deep red seeping through from beneath his jacket.

The blood turns to a sea of sand that consumes all. A strong wind rushes through, transforming the sand into a swirling twister. Ida closes her eyes until the sting from the sand and grit recedes. When she opens them again, she's in an office.

Harper is there, accepting a file from Morelli.

"What's this?" Harper asks.

"A case."

"If you didn't notice, I already have a pretty big one on my hands."

"Listen to me for a minute, Detective." Morelli holds her gaze. "Many moons ago, I remember there being a girl found up at Wisher's Pond. Twenty-four years old, I believe. Anyway, everything about that case bears more than a passing resemblance to your two girls."

Harper opens the file. She reads the name at the front: "Ruby Lane?"

Ida thinks: Mom.

Another shift in time. Morelli's lawn at night.

A gun flashes in the moonlight.

On the grass with his life leaking away, Morelli can feel his heart slowing. His breathing comes in ragged, shallow bursts. Everything is cold, numb. The sky overhead is populated with a billion stars, and the light, the throbbing light, is pulsing, getting stronger, coming, going, coming, going.

Ida feels the tug of the outside. The pull of reality, dragging her back from the confusion of memories and moments that is Captain Frank Morelli.

She screams into the shifting void. Who was it? Who had you killed?

The bond crumbles.

Threads loosening.

Coming undone . . .

Ida staggers back, and Albie catches her in his arms. He lowers her gently to the floor.

"Jeez, are you okay?" he asks in a worried voice.

Ida nods slowly. "Gimme a minute."

Harper goes to Morelli's side, looks at him for a long moment before covering the man back up. She returns him to the cold.

"Harper, I'm really worried about her."

"She'll be fine. Watch the door," Harper says. She hunkers down next to Ida. "Are you okay? Did you get anything?"

Ida hugs herself, staring into space.

Albie opens the door, checks the hall outside.

"Help me get Ida up off the floor," Harper says. They take an arm each and get Ida to her feet. As they walk her to the door and out into the hall, Harper glances back inside the room.

The lights are back on.

14

The boy was now a man, and climbing the ladder fast. Running lead on homicides and home invasions across town—which helped when you had to cover up a murder now and then.

He found love; not just a woman who would kiss him and show him affection because of the paper in his wallet. A woman who would do that because she wanted to, because she felt compelled to touch his face and tell him he needed a shave. A woman who would hold his hand in public, even though she knew public displays of affection gave him the sweats. A woman he didn't have to buy things for, didn't have to shower with money.

Ten years younger than him, hair the color of straw trailing all the way down her back. When Emily was on top of him, making love in her slow, grinding way, her hair fell on either side of him like curtains. All he could see was her face, the smooth white of her neck, her breasts, her hands on his chest. He loved looking at her. At the way her eyes closed when they were having sex. The thin lines of her lips, and the beads of sweat that collected across the top.

With her hand in his, walking down the street at night, heading out for a few drinks, Hope's Peak was a world of possibilities, a place filled with promise. Perhaps that promise was right next to him, her small, fragile hand enclosed by his, her other hand on his upper arm, not just walking next to him but hanging on to him and telling all the world: This is my man. I feel safe and protected when I'm with him. I feel loved.

The surprising thing was, he felt the same way. Sometimes he woke up next to her in the early hours, the phone going off in the hall. Some case or other. He would make his excuses and go back to the bedroom. Instead of getting back into bed next to her, he'd sit on the edge and watch her breathing in her sleep. Reach out to push the hair from her face.

This is a woman I could settle down with. Someone soft, caring, and genuine, who loves me. Isn't that what I've always wanted?

Until the day he drove through Chalmer and saw Emily walking along the street with another man. The detective circled back and followed them as they entered a hotel—more of a bed-and-breakfast, really. He waited for them to go inside, stomach twisting into a knot.

The detective took his hands off the steering wheel, held them up in front of him. They trembled with rage. He got out of the car and walked into the hotel. Flashing his badge, he gave their description to the clerk at the front desk and asked if he'd seen them that day.

The clerk complained that he wasn't meant to divulge who was staying there, but if it was serious, he'd help. "It's serious, alright," he assured him. His hands tingled with pins and needles.

The clerk pointed him in the direction of Room 8. Up the stairs and along the hall.

The detective went up there, one hand on his sidearm. With the other, he hammered hard on the door.

The mystery man answered the door, the bedsheet wrapped around his lower half.

The detective saw red.

Pulled his gun from the holster, shoved it into the man's chest, driving him into the room, kicking the door shut behind him. The backs of the man's legs hit the bed, and he fell back on it, hands up defensively. "What the hell, man? Why do you have a fucking gun?"

The detective looked around. The bathroom door opened and Emily appeared, stark naked in the doorway, her face dull with shock.

Some part of him wanted to scream like a child with rage. The other part of him wanted to ram the gun into the guy and keep pulling the trigger, plugging him with so many holes he resembled swiss cheese.

"Get dressed and get out of here," he told Emily, barely able to move his mouth, his teeth were clenched so tight.

"Please," Emily begged him. She reached slowly for the gun.

The detective lashed out with his left hand, striking the side of her face.

Emily stumbled back, holding her face. Eyes filling with hurt, confused tears. "Why? It's not what you think!"

"Really?" he yelled at her. The man on the bed started to get up, and the detective smashed him in the face with the gun. His nose burst open, blood spilling everywhere. "This sorry sack-of-shit fuck you good and proper, huh?"

"Don't do this!" Emily cried, voice broken with emotion.

"Get out of here," he told her.

Emily hurriedly threw her clothes back on, and when she reached the bedroom door, she turned around. "Will you ever forgive me?"

"No," he spat. "Now get the fuck out of here."

Emily pointed to the man on the bed. "What're you going to do with Charlie?"

Ah. Now I have a name.

"Get. The. Fuck. Out. Of. Here," he growled. He watched Emily leave, then turned back to the man on the bed. "So, Charlie. Do you make it a personal mission to sleep with other men's girls?"

"I didn't realize she belonged to you," Charlie said, hand over his face, blood gushing down his cheeks and dripping from his chin.

"Oh, she doesn't. Nobody does. I don't treat people like they're my fucking possessions."

"Sure don't seem like it," Charlie said.

The detective reached around for his cuffs. "I'm arresting you," he said, throwing them to Charlie. "Snap one of them around your wrist. I'll do the other one."

"What the fuck, man?"

He lifted the gun, brought it down on Charlie's face again. There was a loud crack—a satisfying crack—and Charlie's cheekbone split wide open. A dribble of red ran down the side of his face.

"Do as you're fucking told!"

Charlie cuffed one wrist, then held out his arms so that the second one could be cuffed. With Charlie bound the way he wanted him, the detective dragged him up off the bed.

"Put some fucking pants on, you piece of shit."

While Charlie did as instructed, the detective snooped around. No evidence the two of them had been staying at the hotel. No clothes lying around, no toothbrushes or combs in the bathroom.

"So you book a hotel room just to fuck in?"

"Look, man, it's not like that," Charlie said.

The detective swallowed the poison rising from deep within. The hate compelling him to ram the end of the gun against Charlie's temple and blow his brains out there and then.

"Save it," he snapped. "Outside. And don't make me hit you again. I don't want blood on my shirt."

Out in the parking lot of the hotel, it was quiet. Nobody walking around out there in the heat. He popped the trunk and told Charlie to get inside.

"You're joking!" Charlie said, backing away.

The detective aimed the gun at him. "Get in alive, or I throw you in dead."

"Please, I didn't know she had a man. If I had—"

"If you had, it wouldn't have made any difference," he said flatly. "Now get in the fuckin' trunk."

Charlie climbed in, hugging his knees to fit. The detective slammed the trunk shut.

What are you doing? You've lost your mind, *the little voice in his head told him.* There will be no coming back from this. When Emily tells the story of you walking into that hotel room and holding her lover up at gunpoint . . .

The detective drove along the street, looked to his right, and spotted Emily walking with her arms folded, head down. She didn't even realize it was him until he pulled up next to her and wound the window down. She nearly leapt with fright.

He smiled at her. "Get in the car."

"No," she said, backing away from him. She was a different girl. A frightened, pale imitation of the lover he liked to watch sleeping in their bed, pushing the hair out of her face.

The detective showed her his gun. "Come on, Emily, honey. Get in the car."

She swallowed. Checked up and down the sidewalk, looking for help. For a savior to swoop in at the last minute and get her out of this jam.

There was no one, of course. Just her boyfriend in his unmarked police car.

He patted the passenger seat. "Come on." Watched her walk around the front of the vehicle, open the door, and climb in. He peeled away from the curb without a word, already knowing where he would take them.

The meadow could've been the middle of nowhere for all that it mattered. Emily sat in the car, shaking in the passenger seat. Outside, he leaned into the trunk, helped Charlie out. Walked him around to the front of the car so that Emily could see him.

"Say hello, Charlie."

Charlie's eyes grew wide at the sight of Emily in the front of the car.

"Fuck! Emily! Emily, get out of here—"

The detective took a step back, then another, until he was a good distance from Charlie. Lifted the gun. Took aim.

"There's always a price to pay," he told Charlie. He fired. The shot knocked Charlie back, the bullet bursting through his neck in a plume of scarlet. The detective holstered his piece, walked back to the car.

Emily screamed from the passenger seat, holding the side of her face as if her head were about to fall apart at the seams. Just screaming and screaming and screaming.

Before he could reach the car door to drag Emily out, show her his handiwork, he heard someone choking. He looked back at Charlie, saw his hands clutching his throat, his body writhing about.

Fuck.

This wasn't how he planned it. Not that he had a plan anyway. More like a notion. Drive him out there, kill him in front of her, prove to her how seriously he took their relationship. But as he drove out to the meadow, Emily began to lose her shine. He saw the woman who had pretended to love him. The woman who had acted as if she loved him. Had even told him that she did, only to fuck around behind his back. Was the whole thing one big act? An elaborate con? The whole time, was Emily just some kind of grifter, playing me like a mark?

He boiled with anger. He'd never killed anyone before, and now that he had, he wondered what all the fuss was about.

Charlie wasn't dead.

His eyes were wide, panicked. He rolled about in agony, blood everywhere—pumping from the wound, over his hands. The detective got in close, aimed the gun at his face. Charlie looked at him.

It's different from shooting from afar. Up close, he saw the fear—the knowledge that everything was about to end. He almost stopped himself. Almost lowered the gun and walked away.

But his finger tensed on the trigger, a thunder crack rolled out across the meadow, and Charlie was still. The detective sat on the hood of the car and regarded the body. He went to run his hands through his hair, but stopped midaction.

Looking down at himself, he found he was covered in blood.

At first light, Emily was on a bus out of town.

He never saw her again.

Now, he pours himself a scotch, takes it in one hit—grimacing from the burn—then pours another.

Problems, problems, problems.

Standing by the window, looking through the gaps in the blinds, he watches the street outside. Quiet, civilized, the way a good, honest town should be.

Detective Harper is first and foremost in his mind as the major cause of much of his upset, dredging up the past—bringing it kicking and screaming into the light.

She doesn't get it, and never will. We did what we did for the good of the town . . . I did what I did because it meant protecting what is dear to me. After all, nothing is more important than your family.

He thinks of his father, who once told him: *"From small things, big things one day come."*

I was the small acorn once. It's a long road to becoming the great oak I want to be.

He pours himself another scotch. A few years ago the local theater had put on *The Tempest*, and though he had not been interested in enduring Shakespeare produced by local amateurs, he went anyway. The play had stuck with him ever since. It left its mark on him. He had taken to quoting lines from the play when his mood turned to the dark deeds the town required from him.

"Hell is empty, and all the devils are here."

On these wicked shores, if a man wants to fulfill his vision, to overcome the devils, he has to become the villain.

The bad man.

The monster.

He lifts the glass to the light, eyes filled with its amber luster. Tips his head back, swallowing it in one go. Looks at his hands. So much older now.

The dirt on these hands, he thinks, looking at the lines on his palms. God knows what they're meant to mean. A life lived. A life taken. A life digging rocks out of the ground, or a life of paper cuts from counting money. It's all relative, and at the same time none of it matters.

He turns off the light, heads out the door to his car. Climbs in, turns the key in the ignition, and feels the familiar, steady rumble of the car's engine. He drives through town to the luxury penthouse he has on the shore, where he can rise in the predawn light and take in the ocean, watch the shifting edge of the surf on the dark sand. Rolling in, fading out.

Using a key fob to open the security gates at the front of his penthouse, he gets a chance to look at himself in the rearview mirror. *Getting old. Wrinkles around your eyes. Gray hairs coming through. Piling on the pounds, too.*

"I'm doing okay," he mumbles, driving through the open gates and parking up against the front of the building. *Let someone else bear the burden of protecting this town for decades, and see how they fare.*

Once everything connecting him to Lester Simmons is covered up, he knows it will be over for good. He can move forward. Run a town free of trash, free of trouble—the sunny, smiling paradise of his dreams. One day, his hands will be clean.

15

Yo-bert's is empty when they walk in. They sit at a window table. Ida has Albie's suit jacket around her shoulders, her head against the glass, eyes shut.

"Is she alright?" Albie whispers, eyeing her with concern.

Harper nods. "Just resting. Trust me, she's stronger than she looks."

Albie moves the menus aside to make room for the waitress, who brings a tray of coffee to the table.

"Thanks, hon. Here's your coffee, and your tubs. Just take them to the dispensers when you're ready, and fill 'em up all you want. If you need more spoons, you come ask, okay?"

"Will do," Harper says.

Yo-bert's has been open for six months, and sees a roaring trade. Harper remembers the ice-cream parlors back in San Francisco when she was a kid. Counters filled with metal trays of handmade ice cream—pistachio, coffee, crème brûlée. Anything you could imagine. Now the hipster thing to eat is frozen yogurt in a similarly wacky array of flavors. She counts sixteen dispensers arranged along the perimeter of the store.

The waitress looks at Ida. "Is she okay?"

Ida's teeth chatter. Albie leans across, pulls the jacket a little tighter around her. "She's just cold and tired."

The waitress nods slowly. "Uh-huh."

She leaves.

Harper rolls her eyes. "I thought she'd never go."

"Ida doesn't look too good," Albie says, voice low.

Harper reaches across and nudges Ida with her hand. Her lids raise just enough to see out. Harper shows Ida the coffee. "You should drink something."

Ida reaches out, her hands rattling. Her thin fingers close around the disposable cup, and she lifts it to her lips. "Th-th-thanks."

"It'll pick you up a bit until we get to my place."

Ida shakes her head. "N-n-no need. Just drop me home. I'll be f-f-fine."

"I won't argue with you about this," Harper says. "You can barely string a sentence together."

Albie stirs Sweet'N Low into his coffee. "What possessed you to pick this place, Harper?"

"Don't know," she says with a shrug. "Seemed low-key."

"So he didn't see the killer," Harper says, working through what Ida has told them. "But he *did* have a meeting with Bill Marshall."

"He was shot dead right after," Albie says. "Then Bill Marshall got killed in a drive-by shooting. That's not a coincidence."

Harper's eyes narrow. She sips her coffee. "So Marshall was involved in many of those cover-ups. Staging the crime scenes so that they looked like something else. A retired detective named Lloyd Claymore told Stu and me that the murders were disguised as suicides, death by misadventure, things like that. Because they were happening at random, and the facts obscured the way they were connected, nobody saw the trend."

"They were all black girls," Albie says. "Which leaves Morelli . . ."

"Your captain weren't dirty," Ida says.

Albie sighs. "So if he wasn't, but Marshall was . . . where's the connection?"

Harper flashes back to the parking lot of the Buy N Save. Watching Marshall wave to her, approach from the sidewalk, then get shot down.

Ducking behind her car, glass raining down. "Whoever had them both killed is pretty pissed about the Internal Affairs situation. Whoever it is, they're running scared that their involvement in the cover-ups will be revealed. And while we're sitting around, they could be targeting somebody else. Who knows who else is on their hit list?"

"Hence why Bill Marshall seemed so rattled in Ida's vision," Albie says.

"What's Freehan got everyone working on over there?" Harper asks him.

"Old cases that Marshall and Morelli worked on. I think Freehan is looking for somebody with a grudge. She's not convinced both deaths are related."

"That's madness. Gut instinct alone tells you it's too much of a fucking coincidence."

"Yeah, well . . . I don't think Freehan goes too much on gut instinct, Harper."

Harper drains her coffee. "Ida, there wasn't anything else you saw that might help us out?"

Ida looks down at her coffee, as if she's wrestling with how to answer. Then she looks back up, eyes heavy. "No."

16

Harper throws the lights on, goes to her bedroom where there are two big blankets on top of the wardrobe, and hands one to Ida.

"I don't have hypothermia, sugar," Ida says, wrapping the blanket about her shoulders regardless. "But I'll take it anyway."

"You did so well today," Harper tells her. "I know you found it tough."

"Always is when you're talking to the dead."

Harper takes the other blanket and wraps herself up in it, suddenly cold. "Do you think you're the only one? You know . . . *gifted* like you are?"

Ida thinks for a moment. "I've wondered the same thing for years—could be I'm just a freak of nature."

"You're not that at all, Ida," Harper tells her. "Far from it."

"But what if I *am* the only one?"

"Then that makes your gift all the more special."

Silence stretches out. What's unsaid makes the air in Harper's apartment feel heavy and cloying. Ida clears her throat, and when she speaks her voice wavers, filled with emotion. "I dream about him, you know."

"Oh," Harper says. "I see."

Ida's expression is hard to read. "How 'bout you?"

"The occasional dream about the girls. You know, in those fields with the crowns on their heads. There's probably a lot more, but you know what it's like when you wake up. It all gets murky. You can't really remember what happened, much less what it was all about."

Ida looks at the far wall, her eyes unfocused. "Mine are like real life. He whispers to me. Sometimes he's gone long enough for me to think he's gone for good, then he does something to remind me he's still around."

Harper swallows. "Like make the telephone ring."

"A part of him latched on to me. Stuck around. He might be dead, but he's still very much around."

"Jesus, Ida . . ."

"He'll fade eventually, I'm sure of it," Ida says.

"I'm surprised you didn't mention it right away," Harper tells her.

Ida is distant. "The first time, I was hanging out the washing, went back to the house, to the kitchen, and heard him next to me. He said, 'I'm *ſtill* here' with that lisp of his. It was almost like I could feel his breath on the nape of my neck. And you know what? Maybe I could, sugar . . . maybe I could."

Ida is an antenna, picking up echoes of the past the way a radio plucks songs from the ozone.

"What are you going to do?" Harper asks.

"Move out, like I told you. Settle an old score. Just watch . . . things will get better."

"Settle an old score?"

Ida brushes it off. "Oh, nothin' you should worry about, sugar. By the time I leave that house, everything will be better. One way or the other."

"Why would you leave that house?"

Ida sighs. "Because that old place is absorbent, takin' on all the bad that has happened. He might've latched on to me, but that place is feeding him. Once I'm gone from there, he'll just fade away."

Harper says, "You sound certain."

"What else do I have?"

"Have you looked for a place in town?"

Ida nods slowly. "I've been to see a couple. Nice places. When the house is sold, I'll be able to afford one, with maybe some money left over. Anyway, enough about me. How's that baby doing?"

"Seems okay," Harper says, looking down at the very slight dome of her belly. "Of course, there aren't any kicks or anything yet. So all I really have is . . . well, my feelings, I guess."

"Sure you don't want to know the sex?" Ida asks.

"I think knowing spoils it."

"I'll just keep my mouth shut, then," Ida says, chuckling to herself.

"It's not just that," Harper says. "I think that, after what's gone on, it wouldn't feel special to know. Not right now."

"You mean, all the death and—"

"No, it's more than that. All these victims we deal with. It hits you, when you're having a kid, how all of them are somebody's kids. Daughters. Sons. It makes you think how you would feel if it were your own kid on a slab. Right now, I don't want to think about whether I'm carrying a girl or a boy. Right now, the life inside of me has no identity."

"I know what you mean, sugar. I wonder, sometimes, how things might've played out if my mother had lost me, instead of the other way around. Would she be in my shoes? Livin' the way I am?"

A long moment stretches out between them.

They both jump as the sky outside flashes white. "Shit," Harper says, hand to her chest. She walks to the window and looks out. Thunder rolls overhead, the two of them ducking instinctively. As if the sound were a falling 747 and not an ordinary meteorological occurrence.

Ida gets up, stands next to her as the rain rattles the windows. "Storm's comin'," she says, face lit by another flash of lightning. "Gonna be a bad one."

◆ ◆ ◆

Harper's room is dark, bedsheets cool.

Curled up on her side in the middle of the bed, Harper runs through the names of fellow detectives past and present. How far did the cover-up go—how many of the Hope's Peak PD's finest have dirtied their hands over the years?

If somebody is cleaning house . . . getting rid of anyone who can connect them to this scandal . . . who's next? *And how do I stop that from happening?*

She closes her eyes, falling toward the nothingness of sleep. Lightning bursts outside. Harper snaps awake, eyes wide, heart thudding.

Another crash.

Not lightning—gunshots.

Ida screams in the living room. Harper rolls out of bed. Her holster is draped over the wardrobe door. She stays low, pulls her gun. Holds it to one side and edges toward her bedroom door as another shot explodes inside the apartment with the accompanying sound of shattered glass.

Ida screams again, terrified.

Harper opens her bedroom door and pushes into the living room, hugging the wall to her left, making a quick visual sweep of what's around her.

The front door is intact. Harper scans the living room. The windows are gone—blown inward. Ida is curled into a ball on the other side of the sofa, shaking with fear. Harper moves to the side of the window frame and peers out. The rain and wind obscure the shooter, but she spots him in the shadows cast by the buildings facing her apartment.

Harper dives back, bullets punching the window frame, wood splinters flying.

"Get to the bathroom!"

Ida moves on hands and knees. Harper peeks around the window frame again—the shooter isn't there. Thunder rumbles over town.

Harper runs to the front door, unlocks it, and heads outside. She hurtles down the stairs barefoot, bursting from the entrance of the building. A wall of cold water driven by the fierce wind hits her in the face. Harper blinks the rain from her eyes, looks up the street to where the shooter is running away.

Harper gives chase, feet splashing through the rain. She stops, aims her gun at him, and fires. The shot goes wide. The man breaks to the right, finds cover behind a car. Harper does the same. She waits, panting for breath.

Edges out.

The man fires. Each shot hitting the car. Harper breaks cover, fires back. The man runs across the street. The wind howls. A car engine starts, headlights bursting to life.

Harper stands, fires at the vehicle as it hurtles toward her, its tires screaming on the dark wet asphalt. She throws herself back, narrowly getting out of the car's way. It tears past, taking the corner at speed, disappearing out of sight.

Harper runs back to her apartment, sirens wailing in the distance. She finds Ida in the bathroom. Harper gets down next to her, puts her arms around her. Ida doesn't say anything—just trembles like a frightened animal. Harper holds her tight against her, conscious of the fact that she is soaking wet.

"It's going to be okay," she tells her. "It's going to be okay."

Ramirez looks at the chaos of Harper's apartment. "Shit."

"You're telling me," she says. A paramedic finishes taking her blood pressure. "Look, are we done?"

"I'm not happy," the medic says, freeing her of the black armband. "You should be checked out at the hospital."

"Not this again. I've been checked out once this week. I don't need it twice."

"Fair enough, but you're going against my advice."

"So be it," Harper says, dismissing the man.

The carpet glitters with broken glass. Wind and rain drove into the apartment until makeshift boards could be screwed into place on the windows. The weather moans against the other side, but at least there is no more water entering her apartment.

Place is already ruined.

Ramirez whistles through his teeth. "Can't say I've ever been shot at twice in two days."

Albie appears in the doorway.

"Is Ida okay?" Harper asks him.

"She's in a car outside," Albie tells her. "We took her statement, and she's eager to get home. There's going to be a cruiser posted outside her place for the rest of the night to put her mind at ease."

Harper nods, still in shock.

Albie studies her. "How 'bout you?"

"I'm fine. Once forensics have finished in here, I'm cleaning up this mess."

Albie shakes his head. "No, you're not. You're coming with me."

"Thanks, but no thanks."

"I won't take no for an answer," Albie says. "I've got a couch with your name on it."

Captain Freehan walks into the apartment. She does not look pleased to be there so late. "Detectives. I heard what went down," she says, looking about. "Looks like Mogadishu in here."

"We're alright—" Harper starts to say.

"Oh, you mean yourself and Miss Lane? The presence of your *seer* friend does little to quell my doubts about your sanity, Detective."

"Captain," Albie interjects before Harper's temperature can boil over. "I was about to take Harper to my place."

"Good idea. Until we have a handle on this," Freehan says. "And, Harper? You're proving yourself to be as much trouble as I thought you were. Detective Goode, get Harper away from this crime scene. Let our people work."

Harper looks about helplessly. "What about this place? My home . . ."

"Tomorrow. There's nothing more you can do tonight. Detective Goode, I said get her out of here."

He steers Harper away. "Yes, ma'am."

◆ ◆ ◆

The wind drives the rain up the street, gutters surging with water. Harper has to get in the back of the police cruiser to talk with Ida. "How are you?"

"Little shaken, but that's all," Ida says.

"I'm going to spend the night at Albie's," Harper says. "He told me they're having your place watched. Is that alright?"

"Don't fret." Ida smiles weakly. "I'll be fine."

Harper pats her hand. Smiles. Gets out of the car. She closes the rear door and steps back as it ferries Ida away.

◆ ◆ ◆

Albie's apartment is silent as a tomb.

"Where's Jon?"

"Probably comatose," Albie says, keeping the lights off, ushering her into the living room.

Within minutes he's fixed her up with a spare pillow and a warm blanket.

"I don't know if I can sleep," Harper tells him.

"I wish I could offer you something strong. You know . . . for the nerves, or whatever."

Harper sits on the sofa. "I'll be fine. Thank you," she says. "You didn't need to do this."

"Yes, I did," Albie says. "Do you want a light on?"

Harper shakes her head. Albie leaves her in the living room, pulling the door closed on his way out. She kicks off her shoes, lies back on his sofa, drawing the blanket up around her. She's suddenly very cold. Thinking about what has happened. Worrying about Ida.

We've had one hell of a night.

Harper feels a tingle in her stomach and wonders if it could be the baby.

Her head hums.

The gunshots that tore through the apartment . . . chasing the shooter down barefoot in the rain . . . all a blur.

Back in San Francisco, she'd nearly died pursuing the sexual predator the papers coined The Moth. He had overpowered her. Tried strangling her to death. Would've succeeded, too, if she hadn't been so lucky. As it was, he fled. And later, Harper was able to stop him in his tracks— see to it he lived out his days behind bars.

Her ex-husband, Alex, married her when she was a cop. He accepted the way she was, the kind of career she envisioned for herself. But when she was promoted to detective, everything changed. Her days were long, and her nights were longer.

They spent less time with one another. Alex started talking to her about requesting a transfer, something safer, where her workload would be less. She could spend more time at home. They could start a family.

Alex spoke of children.

The notion of having a child frightened her to death because it meant the stakes were so much higher.

When she nearly died in that alley, there'd been nothing to lose. She never gave Alex a second thought. Nor the future he had in mind for them both. She just put her job first, and let everything else come in second place.

But tonight, with bullets punching holes in her apartment . . . Harper felt the icy hand of fear around her heart. For the first time, there was more at stake. More to lose.

The alley stretched into the darkness.

Harper maintained a low stance, gun held off to one side, clasped in both hands. She went in alone, pulse pounding in her ears.

Steam billowed from a pipe jutting out of a rotten brick wall to her right. The air thick with the smells of cats and overcooked Chinese takeout. Dumpsters arranged haphazardly to one side. Boxes and busted crates on top of them. Trodden, soggy trash.

Harper pressed on, watching for any sign of movement. She'd chased the suspect two whole blocks before he ducked into the alley—one way in, one way out. She was short of breath, chest burning. Legs spent, heavy as stone.

Harper blinked to maintain her focus.

A can tumbled to the ground, the sound of it like the crash of a cymbal. Harper's grip tightened reflexively on her gun. She aimed into the gap between two of the dumpsters. A cat scurried out between her legs, forcing her to leap back.

Something moved in the extreme left of her field of vision. She spun, lifting her gun, ready to aim at whatever was there. The suspect slammed into her, driving her back into the dumpster. Swept the back of her legs, pulling her down. Harper clung onto him, and he shook her off.

Her gun was on the ground. She went for it. The suspect threw himself at her. They rolled together, down on the stinking wet ground. Harper kicking any part of him she could get at.

The Moth was on top. He pulled his arm back, and Harper knew what was coming. She tried to move, but he had her pinned. She flinched as his fist smashed into her face, bouncing her skull off the pavement behind her. Stars exploded in Harper's vision, ears popping, head filled with an electric hum.

Harper forgot her training. The man overpowered her so quickly, and now his hands were on her throat. She bucked her hips, tried to roll from one side to the other. Used all her strength to pull at his arms, but they were locked solid. Hands pushing and pushing on her neck, stopping her from taking a breath. The darkness closing in.

His eyes were black holes that contained nothing. No remorse. No pity. Nothing but the act of forcing the life out of her. Watching dispassionately as Harper choked for breath.

A shot rang out, and The Moth dove back. Harper gulped in big lungfuls of air. Sucking it in, desperate for oxygen. Another shot cracked the night wide open. The suspect took off.

Another gunshot snapped through the alley. The Moth staggered to one side, faltered, then regained his pace. Harper fell back, her head against the cold, wet ground, watching the steam piling up into the empty night.

I'm alive.

She clutched her chest and tried to breathe . . .

Harper thinks about how The Moth cost her her marriage and nearly her life, and Lester Simmons cost her the father of her unborn child. *Why do I pursue these things the way I do?*

Harper's hand goes to her neck. She connected with Lester's victims because they had been strangled to death; she knows from firsthand experience how that feels, having someone on top of you, their hands clamped around your neck. Every passing second the darkness closing in, getting tighter and tighter. The last moments of your life like grains of sand falling toward the abyss.

Harper closes her eyes, and she is back there in the alley. Before Hope's Peak. Before Stu, or Ida, or Lester Simmons. On the cold, wet ground, gasping for breath, the darkness receding. But not caring. Knowing there will be nothing left behind. Knowing what Alex will confirm later, in the emergency room by her bedside.

"I want you to quit."

Harper looked at her hand enclosed within his. "I can't."

"You're going to die," he said, his voice bitter and hurt. "This job will kill you, Jane. I don't want to have to bury my wife."

"That's not going to happen," Harper told him resolutely.

Her husband searched her face for the truth. He didn't find it there.

"You're lucky, Jane," he said, letting go of her hand. Standing. Emotion draining out of his face, and Harper's heart breaking because of it.

I've done this. I've broken him.

"Alex . . . ," she said.

He walked to the door, turned back. Hurt in his eyes. "One day your luck's going to run out. I can't be there to see it . . ."

17

"I think we can command a good asking price," the real estate agent, Michael, tells her. He takes a picture of the kitchen from the doorway, then another from the other end.

Ida watches all of this with bemusement. She's sorted through her belongings as best she can.

"That's good news," Ida says.

Michael nods enthusiastically. "Oh yes. These old fixer-uppers are hot right now."

Ida frowns. "Fixer-upper?"

"Yeah. Someone will come in here, practically rip it all apart, start again. But it's the outside you're selling. The frame. And this is a solid old house. Your inspection came back okay?"

"Yes," she says, a little numb at the thought of someone going in there with a sledgehammer and smashing the place to bits. "No issues with it. Good foundation, and all that."

"Great. Of course, I have a copy of the report on my desk someplace."

He takes a picture of the staircase to the second floor.

"And those apartments I looked at in town?" Ida asks.

Michael grins. "All available. You tell me when you'd like to move in, and we'll get the ball rolling."

Rolling too fast, I think, Ida tells herself. But she says, "Okay," and watches as he continues taking photographs, documenting the place as if it's a crime scene.

"Mind if I head on upstairs and take some more snaps for the site?"

She shakes her head. "Knock yourself out."

"Thanks," he says, running up the stairs two at a time.

Ida sags when he's gone, and goes into the kitchen. She stands against the counter and looks out at the distant tree line, at the dark clouds gathered on the horizon, coiled springs of darkness and foreboding. A strong wind has kicked up from their direction. The morning looks like dusk.

Am I doing the right thing here?

She feels as if it's the only thing she can do, to move on.

Michael thumps down the stairs and pokes his head around the kitchen doorframe. "These pictures will do for now. Ideally, I'd like to come back here when the place is emptied out completely."

"Oh . . . okay," Ida says.

If he thinks the place is full of stuff now, he should've seen it a few weeks ago.

"Alright? And stop by the office, or call my cell, whenever you're ready to take the plunge," Michael says. "Just don't leave it too long. Some of those apartments are hot."

Everything's hot with this guy.

Ida walks him to the door. "Thank you. See you soon."

"Bye."

She's glad when she shuts the door and, seconds later, hears his sports car roar down the lane, leaving a plume of dust in its wake.

Ida looks around the space. It's grown dark outside, and that has robbed the house of any cheerfulness it might have had. Already empty, stark, and bare, it doesn't resemble the house she grew up in. The minimum amount of furniture to get her by until she leaves. Most of her personal belongings in boxes and bags in the back bedroom upstairs.

With only herself for company, it's quiet in here. And now, with it cleared out, there is an empty echo that surrounds her like a vacuum.

Creak.

Ida's breath catches in her throat. She stands where she is by the door and listens.

Creak.

She swallows. Walks slowly, one step at a time—one foot in front of the other—through the living room. That creaking noise isn't the sound of wind hitting the house or floorboards shifting under someone's feet in the middle of the night.

It's the sound a rope makes when it has a heavy load at one end, and it's pulled taut.

She remembers that sound all too well.

CREAK.

Ida holds the banister and climbs the stairs, taking her time, knowing what she will find up there, knowing what awaits her. Her impulse is to run out of the house and come back later. She knows that's not the best way to deal with it. The best way is to acknowledge what is there, and then ignore it. But it's easier said than done sometimes. Ida reaches the top step, and looks down the landing at the second bedroom. There, on the end of the rope, is her grandpappy. As Ida watches, his body swings back and forth like a pendulum, the rope creaking under his weight, the light above him creating a dusty aura around his downturned head.

"I know you're not real," Ida says, her voice little more than a squeak, her left hand gripping the banister so hard it's a wonder it doesn't splinter apart. "Leave me alone."

Her grandpappy's head rises, swollen eyeballs swiveling about. His mouth moves wordlessly. His blackened, swollen tongue flaps against the insides of his teeth, but no sound comes out. Just a weird sucking noise, like a fish trying to pluck a bug from the surface of the water.

Ida is frozen to the spot. She wants to look away, but can't. She wants to cover her eyes, but her arms are heavy as lead. She wants to run, wants to fly, but her feet have become one with the floorboards. "Please," she pleads with him. "Go away. Leave me alone. I don't want this. Please."

His eyes roll into the back of his head, and his mouth opens wide, releasing a swarm of tiny flies that sizzle against the light over the landing, dissolving into smoke upon contact with the light bulb. Finally, Ida is able to close her eyes. When she opens them again, her grandpappy is gone. There is no rope creaking. Just dust swirling in the doorway where he had been seconds before.

Ida takes a deep breath, heads down the stairs, and goes outside, needing some fresh air. She walks onto the porch as rain begins to pitter-patter on the timbers.

18

There is an officer on watch outside her apartment door.

"Hey," Harper says, showing him her ID. "These two guys are with me. They're gonna fix the place."

"Sure," he says, moving out of their way.

"Thanks. Do you want me to make you a coffee or something?" Harper asks, letting the two repairmen into the apartment first.

The officer shakes his head. "No, thanks, ma'am. I'm fine."

"Okay."

The owner of the building was told about the shooting the night before. Earlier that morning, Harper's cell rang. It was the landlord, telling her that he would have two men outside her apartment within the hour, ready to get to work.

"Really?" Harper had asked him. "There's not a huge rush."

"Oh yes there is," he said. "You're my most famous tenant!"

She got showered, dressed, and left Albie's apartment as soon as possible. Caught a cab back across town to her apartment building where, true to the landlord's word, the two repairmen were waiting. Standing against their dusty van, smoking.

Harper leaves them to do their thing, can hear them talking among themselves in her living room. Walking into the kitchen, there is a blackened hole to her right where a bullet punched into the wall. It knocked a picture off, which sits facedown on the floor. Harper bends down, picks it up. All of the glass is smashed. It tumbles out of the frame, over the floor, cutting her finger in the process.

"Fuck," Harper hisses, setting the empty picture frame on the kitchen counter and going to the sink. She runs her fingertip under the cold water, then finds the first-aid box. She wraps a bandage around her finger, cursing under her breath.

The picture inside the frame is unblemished. Harper goes to it, turns it over, and unclips the back, slipping the photograph out. She holds it in her hands, looking at it, secretly thankful that it is unharmed.

When she first got partnered with Stu Raley, they worked a case together: a local man had murdered his wife, leaving her body on their living room floor and performing a disappearing act. They tracked him down and arrested him, but during the investigation Harper got the news that her father had died. She traveled out of town to attend the funeral, and at the wake, her stepmother handed her a shoe box of old photographs, letters, things like that. A jumbled collection of mementos from a life Harper had wanted no part of.

The photo from the frame is black-and-white. Harper is five years old, on her father's shoulders. They're both smiling.

It's weird. I don't remember smiling all that much as a kid, Harper thinks.

She looks back down at the photo. A happy time she doesn't remember. She wishes she could. It was here, in this very kitchen, that she told Stu what had happened. That her father had died.

This apartment has a lot of memories. It's my own shoe box of good times, bad times, regrets, and new beginnings. I guess me and Dad had something in common, after all.

She opens one of the cupboards, puts the photo in there for safe-keeping. Last night on Albie's couch, the gunshots still ringing in her ears, Harper couldn't help but think of Bill Marshall. The way he died. She'd very nearly suffered the same fate—twice.

Harper knows all too well that she has been targeted through association. Through the misfortune of being present in the wrong place at the wrong time. Harper tells the two repairmen that she is leaving for a few hours, and then tells the officer guarding her front door. Harper has never been one to sit on her hands when everything goes to shit around her. Better to be a participant than a spectator. But in this case, better to be a *participant* with no spectators . . . and the best way to accomplish that is to wait for the cover of night.

◆　◆　◆

"The captain has been dead forty-eight hours," Freehan says. Ramirez and Albie are seated on the other side of the desk, alongside Detective Clara O'Hare. "So what have we got?"

"I've been looking into the captain's time in New Orleans," O'Hare says.

Ramirez looks sideways at her. "I didn't know he did a stint down in the Big Easy."

"Neither did I," O'Hare says. "But he was there about three months."

"Anything from it?" Freehan asks.

O'Hare exhales. "Not yet. He went down there to assist in an op to put some notorious gunrunners behind bars. Far as I can tell, there were no threats of reprisals."

"So a dead end, in other words," Freehan says, her voice sharp.

O'Hare blushes.

Freehan turns her gaze to Albie and Ramirez. "How about you two? Turned up any possible assholes who might be responsible for killing the captain?"

"Before he made captain, Morelli busted this guy for dealing crystal. Louie Richards."

"Go on."

"Well, Louie wasn't dealing it. He was *supplying* it," Ramirez says. "Fucker didn't cook it, just got hold of it. Fished it out."

Freehan nods. "A middleman."

"Yeah. So he busts him for that, and the guy admits to it. But at the same time, his wife finds out he's been sleeping with one of his pushers. A young girl, much younger than him." Ramirez smirks. "Pretty as all hell."

"Then what happened?" Freehan asks.

"While he was being sentenced, his wife went and killed that young girl. Shot her in the face, then turned the gun on herself."

Albie swallows. "Jesus."

"Toxicology found the wife's system full of meth. It seems he was supplying her with it, too."

"But that's got nothing to do with Morelli," Albie says, frustrated at his inability to see the connection Ramirez is making.

"If Louie Richards wasn't caught for distributing crystal, his wife wouldn't have found out about him fuckin' that girl. The murder-suicide might not have happened."

Freehan says, "I take it nothing happened in the end?"

"Louie was locked up. His wife was buried, as was the girl he was stepping out with. But what's relevant is that Louie was told, halfway through his sentencing hearing, about what had happened. I still remember, clear as day, him turning to Morelli and promising him that he'd get him," Ramirez says. "He swore on that bench that he'd pay."

"And you think he waited all this time?" O'Hare asks.

"I don't know. It's a possibility. I kind of forgot about the whole thing until we were looking through Morelli's old cases and came across it."

"And what about Bill Marshall?"

Albie shifts in his seat. "Sifting through his cases now. No recent parolees. Nothing else that leaps out. Marshall's been retired for a few years already, so why wait to seek revenge until now? Are we considering that the killer might not have targeted Morelli and Marshall specifically, but is targeting detectives in general? The media gave a lot of attention to the Simmons case and the possibility that his older murders were covered up by—"

"One thing at a time, Detective," Freehan interrupts. "Ballistics on the bullets that killed the captain and Bill Marshall?"

Albie sighs. "Two different guns. No matches in the database with the bullets we pulled from Morelli's crime scene. Or those that killed Bill Marshall. So we're not going to find a link between the guns and Marshall's and Morelli's cases since ninety-five—that's as far back as we've digitized. Both guns were nine millimeter, though. The same with the shots fired at Jane Harper last night, though that one had no silencer," he adds. "Completely different weapon. Again, no matches on file."

"Unusual," Freehan says. "We can conclude the shooter was a professional because of the silencer. Apart from last night. That was different. The attack on Harper's apartment was meant to be loud. Whoever is behind it, they wanted to scare her."

Ramirez clears his throat. "Could be a guy who's tossing the weapon each time. Trying to make it harder for us to prove a connection between each incident. Just a hunch," he says, shrugging.

Freehan looks from Ramirez to Albie. "I don't go much on hunches, Detectives. I go by facts, and right now, apart from a few paper-thin leads . . . we don't have many."

Albie consults his notepad. "I checked the traffic cameras to see if we could trace the car that drove away from Harper's residence, but it's a dead end."

"How so?"

"It took a route through town that, for one reason or another, is uncovered by traffic cams."

Freehan sits back. Rubs her face. "So what you're saying is, it vanished."

"What I'm saying is that whoever drove the car knew what route to take," Albie says. "They knew what streets were covered by cameras, and avoided them."

"Clever," O'Hare says.

Freehan looks at the three of them. "Well, keep at it. But we really need to get a break in this case. A lead. Anything. Okay, that will be all," she says, then when they get up to leave: "Hang back a moment, Detective Goode."

"Sure," he says, noticing the look Ramirez is giving him as he escapes.

O'Hare and Ramirez leave the room, and Freehan gets up from the desk, closes the door behind them. "I don't want tongues wagging," she tells him. "How is Detective Harper?"

"Fine, I think. Considering."

Freehan sits back down. "And where is she now?"

"I don't know."

She taps her fingers against her desk. "Listen, Detective Goode. I want to know if Harper has told you anything about visiting Morelli's widow."

"I didn't know anything about it. Where are you going with this?"

Freehan's face tightens. "Your friend needs to be careful, Detective. When I tell someone to stay away from an investigation, I really mean it. Pass that on for me, if you happen to see her later today."

"I will."

"Last thing I need is someone who employs fast-and-loose investigative methods," Freehan continues. "Using that psychic to gain insight into the victims' lives. Our work is built on a foundation of facts. Science. Psychology. Something we can convince a jury *actually* happened. Not the ramblings of a madwoman. Especially the grieving daughter of a victim who was likely using Harper for her own revenge."

Albie remembers Ida Lane pressing her hands to Morelli's ice-cold skin. He shakes his head. "Ida Lane helped Harper get a lead on the Simmons case."

"You can't see how this psychic might have been using Harper to enact vengeance?"

"Honestly? No."

Freehan frowns. "I'll tell you, I see bad practices here, Detective. According to IA, a half dozen of the most decorated lawmen in this town have something linking them to corruption in the Simmons case. You know what that means, Albert. Bribes. Extortion. Things like that."

"Not Morelli," Albie says.

"To be determined. Personally, my theory is that he was in it up to his neck. He knew things that IA would uncover, given enough time, and whoever killed him was frightened about what he'd give up to save himself. Maybe the same with Marshall. And if they manipulated evidence in one case, then every case is suspect."

"With all due respect, the man is dead!" Albie snaps, outraged.

"Yes. And why do you think that is, Detective? Do you really think he didn't have some connection to the corruption that has tainted this department?"

Albie looks down.

"Look, from what I've seen, Morelli was a good captain," Freehan says. "But having knowledge of it makes him just as guilty. Turning a blind eye to crime is as bad as being a criminal yourself."

"You're wrong about him," Albie says.

Freehan sighs. "Anyway, regardless of what I believe, I want Morelli's killer found and brought to justice. Tell Harper I won't have this investigation called into question because of the kind of company she is determined to keep."

"I don't know what Harper is up to, if anything," Albie says. "She stayed at my place last night. Apart from that . . ."

Freehan gives him a look. "I am going to tell you this straight, so there can be no confusion. If Jane Harper tries to enlist your help, you will refuse and come see me. If you suspect her of investigating off the record, you will come see me and tell me what you know. My role here is to guide the ship through stormy waters. And when we get to the other side—and we will—I will ensure corruption and bad practice has no place in this police department."

"Understood," Albie says.

"I have nothing personal against Detective Harper," Freehan tells him. "But this psychic nonsense is just that—nonsense. I've made that clear to her. Now I'm making it clear to you. Stick with Ramirez, and give Harper a wide berth."

Albie nods. "Of course."

19

Ramirez leans against the roof of the car, smoking a cigar. From a distance he really *does* look like Sam Elliott. Thick white 'stache, the trail of smoke rising from his slightly parted lips. Albie isn't sure what an older man like Ramirez thinks of getting paired with him.

Decades younger.

Black.

Gay.

Albie's seen his fair share of discrimination since joining the force—backhanded comments about being a "faggot" and a "queer"; intimidation from senior colleagues; the suggestion, mostly from the older males, that he is not as masculine because of his sexual orientation. It wouldn't surprise him if Ramirez harbored the same kinds of misgivings about being his partner.

But when he reaches the car, Ramirez smiles and Albie's doubts retreat to the back of his mind. "You okay?" Ramirez asks.

"Yeah. Just getting chewed out by Maleficent."

Ramirez nods, removes the cigar from his mouth. Stubs it out on the hood of the car. The two of them get into the car.

Albie knows about Ramirez's home life. His wife. His kids. All grown up now and moved away. And Ramirez always has a story to tell. Cases he's worked on. Close shaves he's had.

"You take your licks and keep going," Ramirez says.

"What does that even mean?" Albie asks, shaking his head.

Ramirez smirks. "Like the time I cornered a thief and got stabbed in the thigh—still hauled the punk into the station, even with the blood collecting in the boots I liked to wear back in those days. You gonna tell me what she said or not?"

Albie reverses out, then heads for the parking lot exit. "She wants me to report on Harper."

"I see."

Albie looks at him. "You don't think it's wrong?"

"I've learned the hard way, so take it from me. Best to keep your head down, son. Let others deal with their own problems. Me and you are partners. We gotta look out for each other. It's the way it is."

"Don't know if I can just leave her to it," Albie says. He does not add that he already helped her; that he's seen Ida Lane's abilities at work in person . . . that they scared and exhilarated him in equal measure. And despite that, he is still conflicted about Ida. He wants to believe what he thinks he witnessed in the morgue, but common sense keeps screaming that it didn't happen. Trust the facts. Trust what your eyes see.

But sometimes you've gotta trust what you feel.

"Friend or no, that girl will land you in deep water," Ramirez warns him. "You're best staying well away from anything she's got herself mixed up in."

◆ ◆ ◆

The house is the American Dream distilled into bricks, mortar, and timber. Clean lines, windows shining without a blemish, and an enticing front lawn. A garage to one side, with a muscle car parked in front of it.

"Louie Richards," Ramirez says, peering out at the house from inside the car. "Doesn't look like the kind of place an ex-con would live, does it?"

"I guess not," Albie says, shutting off the engine, wondering how you can generalize about the kind of place an ex-con would live. He certainly never would have considered the possibility that someone might leave prison and have enough money to live somewhere half-decent.

"Scumbag."

"What did this guy do? I was surprised when you threw him out as a possibility for our shooter."

"How so?"

"It's not usually your style to offer up suspects. You're more of a sit-at-the-back-of-the-room type of guy."

Ramirez grimaces. "I don't like being the center of attention. That's all. But this is our captain. Gunned down on his own front lawn. It's a fuckin' travesty."

"Do you really think this guy might have pulled the trigger on Morelli?" Albie asks.

"Dunno. But we can't just mope around at the office. This is the only lead I have right now. It's worth checking out."

"True enough," Albie says.

Ramirez gets out of the car. "Shall we?"

The pair approach the house. Ramirez stands to one side as Albie rings the bell a few times. Albie is about to ring it again when the door opens.

"Yeah?" a bald man wearing dark-blue jeans and a black vest fills the doorway with his considerable frame.

Albie holds his ground. "Louie Richards?"

"What's it to you?"

Ramirez shows him his badge. "Detective Ramirez. This here is Detective Goode."

"What's this about?" Louie asks, scowling at them both.

"We'd like to ask you a few questions," Ramirez says. "Can we come inside?"

"No, you can't." He doesn't budge from the doorway. "Anything you want to ask me, you can ask me from there. The doorstep. That's as far as you guys are getting."

"Fair enough," Albie says.

"Where were you the night before last?" Ramirez asks, as Albie takes notes on his smartphone with a stylus.

Louie shakes his head as if it's full of fire ants. "No, no, no. I'm not doing this. I haven't been in trouble with the law for years. Where is this coming from?"

"There's been a major incident, and we're attempting to identify the person, or persons, responsible," Ramirez says, his voice neutral.

Louie smacks a fist against his palm. "Doesn't matter what I do, I can't ever get past it with you guys, can I?"

"How do you mean?" Albie asks.

"A man does his fuckin' time, comes out, stays on the straight and narrow . . . and all I get is harassed. Cops calling at my door, asking me a bunch of questions. Some crime's been committed? A victim got shot. It was on the TV. Well, read my lips, will you? It's got nothing to do with me."

Ramirez's eyes narrow. "The victim was Captain Frank Morelli. I believe you're familiar with that name."

Louie stiffens. "Some."

Ramirez laughs. "That all you got to say?"

Louie advances toward him, all muscle and agitation. "Yeah. It is. That a problem?"

"You made death threats when Morelli was a detective, working your case. Do you deny that?"

"Of course not. I mean, look at me. Do I look the same as that little dick selling crystal meth years ago? I'm a different man now."

Ramirez runs a hand over his mustache. "Do you own a gun?"

He hesitates. "Yeah."

"Got a license?"

"Of course, man, what d'you take me for?"

Albie says, "An ex-con."

"Where is it?" Ramirez asks before Louie can react to Albie's comment.

"Let me go get it . . . ," he says, turning away.

Ramirez bounds forward, hand on his sidearm. "Stop right there, sonny. If you go inside that house to retrieve a weapon, we'll have no choice but to detain you, or put a bullet in you. You might not get much say as to which one."

"Don't you want to see it?"

Albie says, "Take us inside. Show us that you have it under lock and key, and we'll come out here to finish our business."

Louie chews this suggestion over before finally nodding. They follow him through to his bedroom. The whole place is modern, nicely decorated. Clean and stylish.

He really did turn things around, Albie thinks. *But then, drug dealers can have nice homes, too.*

Louie opens a walk-in closet and reaches for the top shelf.

"That's enough," Ramirez tells him. "Get back and let us do the honors."

"It's in that metal lockbox up there. That's it, behind the golf clubs."

Ramirez pushes the clubs to one side, revealing the lockbox behind them. He carefully pulls it down and lays the box on the end of the bed. "D'you mind?" he asks Louie.

"Not at all."

Ramirez examines the box. "Pretty sturdy. You got the key for the lock?"

"Oh yeah," Louie says. He reaches inside his shirt and lifts a key on a chain. He pulls it over his head and hands it to Ramirez.

"Curious way of carrying the key to a lockbox," Ramirez says. "For a guy who doesn't use what's inside it."

"So where were you three nights ago, Mr. Richards?" Albie asks him.

Louie folds his arms. "At a watering hole in town. The Gator Snap?"

"Really?" Albie asks, glancing at Ramirez. "You know that's a cop joint, right? We can check that out."

"Be my fucking guest," Louie says.

"No need to cuss. I'm just doing my job."

Louie scowls. "It's my fuckin' home. I'll cuss all I want."

"What were you doing at the Gator Snap?" Albie asks him, writing it down.

"Playing guitar."

"For real?"

"Sure. I picked it up in prison. Discovered I have a bit of talent. A buddy of mine told me they were looking for a guitar player at the Gator Snap a couple of nights a week."

"So there will be witnesses to corroborate that you were there."

"Probably some of your cop friends," Louie says.

Another dead end, Albie thinks. "What time did you leave?"

Louie scratches the side of his temple. "About two in the morning? Somethin' like that."

"Right. How about you let me see that license," Albie says.

Louie busies himself going through his drawers in the bedroom, looking for the license. Albie watches him to be sure he doesn't try something, like pull a weapon from one of the drawers.

Meanwhile, Ramirez opens the box. "Shit."

Albie looks over.

Ramirez shakes his head. "Wrong caliber." He shuts the box in disgust. "Come on."

Louie gives Albie the license. Albie checks it over and hands it back to him. "Thanks for your assistance. You can put your weapon away now."

Louie stands there, arms open. "That's it? Really?"

"Really," Albie tells him.

Outside, Ramirez lights a cigar. "I thought he was our guy. He had motivation and everything."

"He'd have to be all kinds of stupid to use a cop bar as his alibi if he was lying. I'll call 'em to confirm his story, but I don't expect anything to come of it."

"Our shooter used a silencer in each instance, and he wouldn't have one of those sitting out for the world to see, either," Ramirez says, squinting at Albie in the bright daylight.

"Seems pretty set up here," Albie says, opening the car door. "Must be telling the truth about being a reformed man, huh?"

Ramirez snorts. "That'll be the day."

20

The girl lay under the Spanish moss.

Hands tied behind her back. Her dark skin discolored slightly where she was bound at the wrists and ankles.

The noose was tight around her neck, cutting in . . . but her face was peaceful.

Serene, almost.

The detective smoked a cigarette. He'd lost the mustache—when he'd started to get a few strands of gray in it, he'd decided it had to go. He dyed the hair on his head; in the space of only a few years, the gray little fuckers were sprouting all over the place. But dyeing a mustache seemed ridiculous to him.

The detective dropped the cigarette, stubbed it out on the grass with the toe of his shoe. Then he thought better of it and bent down, picking up the butt and putting it in his pocket to get rid of later.

The call came in, said that there was the body of a young woman in the field just outside Hope's Peak. The detective said he would go check it out.

He went alone.

"Probably another hoax," he'd said, referring his colleagues to an incident six months before, in which a body had turned out to be a mannequin dumped at the back of a health food store, its legs poking out from behind a dumpster. "I'll go take a look, call it in if it's real."

The owner of the field, a farmer by the name of Jake North, wanted to go with him, but the detective shook his head. Told him to remain at his farmhouse and keep people out of the field. It could disturb the evidence. Sure that he was alone, he drove out here, following a dirt track that Jake North used to access the endless rows of corn, now turning dry in the heat.

Sure enough, there was a girl there. A crown of supplejack around her head. Raped and strangled. The life wrung out of her. The detective sat down in the dirt next to her, pondering his next move.

Another body. Another headache. He'd become a professional at fixing things for his half brother.

The detective went to his car, took the sheets from the trunk, and carefully wrapped up the young woman's body, tying them with cord to keep them in place. He carried her to the trunk. Luckily she was small. Petite. He didn't need to contort her in any way to make her fit. He kicked the dirt around out there to disturb the crime scene. Hide any evidence from Farmer North. After putting her in the trunk, the detective drove to the farmhouse and informed North there was nothing out there.

"One of my men saw it!" North said, eyes wild. "He swears there was a girl out there! Flat out on the ground."

The detective shook his head. "Sorry, but there was nothing there. Maybe he imagined it. Which man was it?"

"Julio," North said, pointing to one of the migrant workers leaning against a fence on the other side of the farm, watching their exchange.

The detective leaned in. "You know, these Mexicans . . . they're into all kinds of shit. Who knows what he's been smoking, huh?"

He drove around, looking for a suitable spot. Somewhere to stage what he had planned. How to portray the girl's death as a suicide, or an accident, took some skill—which he'd acquired since becoming aware of Lester and his macabre tastes. When he saw a gathering of trees out in the middle of a field, Spanish moss hanging from their long, muscular branches, he knew he'd found the right spot. Checking that the coast was clear, that there were no vehicles coming his way, no walkers with their dogs, or farmhands, the detective set about hanging the young woman from the tree.

He made it look like a hanging, and left it to the imagination of the investigating detectives to decide if she'd killed herself or had her head forced into the noose. To cover for one mystery, he created another.

Now, watching her sway, the detective couldn't help the pang of regret he felt in his gut, where it hurt. He'd hardened up over the years. But there was still that part of him, a soft center, that got bruised now and then. When he dealt with the mess Lester left behind, he had to fight the impulse to go put a bullet in the bastard's head. Or haul him down to the station and get him to confess.

The detective gave it a day, then called it in, pinching his nose so that his voice sounded higher pitched, more nasally. He described the girl hanging from the tree, and where it was, then hung up. Next he collected prints of the photographs he shot the day before. Black-and-whites from a lab out of town.

Later that evening, after work, the detective dropped by the nursing home, where his father sat in a chair by the window in his room, watching the green sky darken. He'd not fully gone—there was someone in there still, knocking about like a marble in a Coke bottle. He was not a blank slate. Not yet.

"Son?" he croaked.

The detective removed the photographs from the envelope and showed them to his father, one by one. The old man's bottom lip trembled, a tear swelling in his left eye until it was fat and heavy, rolling pitifully down his bony cheek.

"Why do you show them to me?"

The detective grit his teeth, leaned forward. "So you know," he snarled. Leaving the room, he shoved the photos inside his jacket pocket. He did this with every victim, so the old man knew . . . and understood what he had left him with.

Later, when his father was completely bedridden and nonresponsive, the detective sat by his bedside, verbally detailing each crime scene, each victim he had to dirty his hands dealing with. Each young, beautiful life snuffed out by Daddy's biggest mistake.

Knowing that, somewhere in there, Daddy was listening.

21

The Hope's Peak Police Department building is quiet. The night shift is in full swing, meaning that most of the offices are dark. The lights are on over the entrance. In a town like Hope's Peak, there is a graveyard shift of about a dozen cops on rotation at any one time.

Rain batters the building, lancing in from one side. It stings her face as she runs—soaking her through in a matter of seconds.

It is easy for Harper to sneak in unseen, using her ID card to swipe herself through without having to check in with the guy manning the front desk, his head buried in a paperback novel.

She fixes herself a coffee before heading down to the basement—doctors be damned if she's pregnant and in need of caffeine.

That late at night, the basement assumes an eerie quality. It is dark, and she can hear pipes creaking as the wind whips outside. Harper pushes her wet hair out of her eyes, takes a sip of coffee, and gets to work.

It was essential she come here when it was quiet. When Freehan would not be here. Her ID card may register if someone goes searching for late-night sign-ins, but that's a risk she is willing to take.

Before Internal Affairs got involved, Harper had the foresight to make copies of the files Morelli had entrusted her with—the secret files Lloyd Claymore kept over the years, locked in a filing cabinet in the basement. She knew that they would be confiscated and that she would likely not have access to them again for a long time.

So she spent an afternoon photocopying every account contained in the file. All of Claymore's work.

Harper removes the file from behind the cabinet where she's hidden it. She opens it, starts at the beginning. Ruby Lane's murder was the launching pad for what would come. The next girl—Lester's second victim, in 1987—was found on the beach. Below a detail of the crime scene, Claymore has written in his barely legible scrawl: *Identified as Odetta Draw.*

There are no pictures, just a written description of the way Odetta was found.

Feet in the surf, laid out on the sand with her arms above her head. There was a crown of twisted vines on her head, but it'd fallen to one side, so was lopsided on her forehead. By the looks of things, this girl was strangled, raped, just the same as Ruby Lane.

Harper goes to the rolling filing cabinets, knowing exactly what she is looking for. Any file predating 1995 has yet to be digitally transferred to the station's computer system. The cabinets hold thousands of records, but because Harper's search is specific, it takes a matter of minutes to locate Odetta Draw's official file. IA have taken copies of these files but left the originals in place—otherwise, her search would be futile.

The attending officers are listed as Lloyd Claymore, Hal Crenna, Bill Marshall. It's not a surprise—she and Stu saw these names when Morelli first shared the files. But at the time, their concern was preventing the killer from claiming another victim. There hadn't been a reason to question anyone but Lloyd.

Bill Marshall's description of the crime scene tells Harper how this particular victim's cause of death was obscured.

Victim was found on the beach, facedown in the water. From the condition of her body, we have surmised that she died from drowning. There are no indications that there was foul play involved.

The coroner at the time, Kris Paszek, concurred with their theory. He found water in her lungs and other factors that established drowning as cause of death. This raises a red flag for Harper.

Harper moves to the computer. Runs a search for Kris Paszek.

Deceased.

Of course he would be.

The next girl, in 1989, Claymore describes puncture marks on her neck, from a needle. She was found in a ditch at the roadside, left exactly the same as Ruby Lane and Odetta Draw.

Raped.

Strangled.

Crowned.

She was never identified.

It's my belief this young girl was a traveler. Maybe she was stopping in town for a few nights before moving on some- where else. The killer saw an opportunity and struck. So far, we haven't had a misper with a girl of her description. She remains a mystery. For now I will label her Jane Doe.

Harper looks for Jane Doe's file from 1989. Finds it, no problem. Again, the attendees are Claymore, Crenna, and Marshall. There is no mention of puncture marks from a needle. Or a crown. Or anything else that thematically links Jane Doe to the first two girls.

Of course, if they recorded evidence of needle punctures, then toxicology would have had to run tests. It would flag that the killer was using drugs to sedate his victims. Stop them from fighting.

Once again, Dr. Kris Paszek backed up their falsified report.

Victim was early twenties. Found by the side of the road. I have determined that she drowned on her own vomit. Excessive alcohol would have caused her to pass out, and in her sleep, her vomit would have obstructed her breathing.

"I'm beginning to really dislike Dr. Paszek," Harper mutters, lifting her coffee to take a sip. She hears movement from upstairs and freezes, poised to take action should somebody be coming downstairs. But the noise passes. She relaxes.

Turns to the next file.

On and on like that, all night long.

She leaves before dawn as the sky adopts a soft yellow hue. When she returns to her apartment, the majority of the damage caused by the shooter has been repaired. She locks the door, strips out of her clothes, and collapses into bed, more certain than she's been since Marshall's death of what she has to do next.

22

The old woman extends a bony, liver-spotted claw of a hand, and Mayor Hal Crenna takes it in his own. Cameras click and flash around him as he comforts her, nods at all the right times as she relates to him the nature of her illness. Heart failure. She has a monitor on the other side of the bed and a tube running up her nose; the table holding the remnants of a hospital breakfast has been pushed aside.

"It really . . . means so much . . . you comin' here . . . to . . . visit me," she tells him, short of breath. She seems to suck in a great lungful of air each time she breathes, but gets nothing from it. As if the air itself is thin—lacking oxygen.

Hal smiles. Pats the back of her hand. "It's my pleasure, Miss Dufresne. I do hope you'll have family dropping by today."

"Later on," she says, her eyes swimming with tears. "They got to . . . work."

"That's good to hear," Hal says. He glances at the cameras. The couple of reporters with them, recording the whole visit to Hope's Peak General. "Honest, hardworking folk of this town, doing their duty, payin' their taxes. I have the utmost respect for their convictions, Miss Dufresne, and quite frankly, I applaud them."

She wipes her cheek as an errant tear forms at the corner of her eye, rolling down her face.

"You're such . . . a good man . . . Mr. Mayor."

He leans forward. "Just Hal to you."

She blushes. If it's possible for an ancient woman dying of heart failure to turn red with embarrassment, that's what happens. She has to look away, smiling for the first time since he dropped by her hospital bed. Making the rounds at the hospital, press in tow, meeting the sick and dying.

Doing his part.

"I'll see you later on, missus," Hal says, patting her hand once again and rising from his seat.

"God bless you!" Miss Dufresne calls after him.

The press moves out of his way, like the Red Sea parting for Moses. They follow him out into the hall. Hal has no suit jacket on. No tie. Just a light-blue shirt, rolled up at the sleeves—the oldest politician's trick. Make it look like you're cooperating, make it appear as if you are there to work, to dig in shoulder to shoulder with the "little people." Loosen the collar. Go casual—apart from the obligatory, oh-so-presidential US flag pinned to your breast pocket.

Hal tucks the back of his shirt into his trousers as the cameras roll. As microphones hover in front of his face.

One of the reporters, a thirtysomething blonde from the local news channel, is the first to throw a question his way.

"What do you get from these visits?"

One side of Hal's mouth lifts in a lopsided grin. "Apart from fulfilling my promise during the election that I would be a mayor for every man, woman, and child in this town, regardless of age, economic status, or social standing?"

"I guess . . ."

"Let me tell you," Hal says, shifting on his feet, feeling the wave coming. "My position is defined by two obligations. Now, don't forget that I am not a stranger to holding this kind of post. As the former captain of the Hope's Peak Police Department, I felt the same obligations, and those are to the electorate and to God. The people of this town—people like Miss Dufresne in there—have voted me into office. They have faith in me, faith that I will deliver on what I promised. They have put their trust in these hands."

Hal shows them his palms, as if they are the roughened hands of a manual worker.

"I owe it to the people of this fine town, to know what they're dealing with. To see, firsthand, the sick in the hospital. The men and women who operate this place are some of the finest doctors and nurses in the country, providing top-class care to our citizens. I not only owe my time, and my energies, to the patients here, but to the professionals providing round-the-clock care, too," Hal says, eyes flicking from one camera to the next. Demanding their attention. "The saints of Hope's Peak. We owe them our all."

Ida watches as the mayor emerges from the hospital waving to reporters, grinning away as if he's not capable of any other expression but mock pleasantness.

"Today," he announced, the sound bite playing over the radio while he was still in there, "the Crenna Foundation, which I started a little more than a year ago, is making a sizable donation to this very hospital. Enough to purchase another six beds for those who need them, easing the strain on our hospital's already limited resources."

Applause rose up around him.

"Dirty bird," Ida says from inside the cab of her truck, fingers angrily clicking the steering wheel. His voice makes her blood run cold. She can hear the similarity to the voice that haunts her dreams, only there is no lisp.

"Thif if me, Ruby."

Crenna trots down the steps, pauses so that a local college girl can snap a selfie with him, then he's off to his private car, parked curbside.

She watches as the mayor's car pulls away and resists the urge to follow it.

I should just tell Harper what I saw in that vision. Tell her what I learned.

But she can't. When Harper brought her the iced tea, Ida nearly blurted it out to her, but she thought better of it. She wanted so much to reveal what Lester's dying mind had shown her.

"I've known about you for a while. I'm your half brother."

The man who presents himself to the people of Hope's Peak as their savior—Honest Hal—and pretends to have their best interests at the heart of everything he does. He is the man Ida has grown to hate.

It should've been so simple. Lester got killed, and finally I could lay my mother to rest. But nothing ever plays out like that. I can't leave my mother in the past. Can't let her move on. Not while that man is walking free. Lester may have done the actual killing, but his half brother, Hal, enabled him. Let him get away with it all that time. The only way to put him behind bars is to tell Harper.

Yet she cannot bring herself to do that. Because then it is Harper who gets the satisfaction of confronting Hal Crenna with his crimes. Making him account for his evils.

The other way—the way she dreads, but knows is inevitable if she is to ever find peace—has her scared.

She drives toward Chalmer in order to find a phone and make a call.

23

The mayor of Hope's Peak waits on the doorstep, water cascading from the edges of his umbrella. He watches the color rush to the woman's cheeks and offers his hand.

"Good morning, Mrs. Raxter," he says, looking around as if unaware of how he arrived on her doorstep—beamed down from orbit, perhaps—only now remarking on the torrential rain. "A rather *gray* morning, but a fine one, if I say so myself."

"Yes, yes, it is," Mrs. Raxter says, grinning, overcome with excitement at his presence. She slips her hand inside his, and Hal lifts it to his mouth, presses his lips against the back of it, all the while maintaining eye contact.

"I wish this were just a courtesy call, Mrs. Raxter. But I'm here to see your husband. Is Gil in, by any chance?"

"Yes, he's in his den. Watching last night's game. He recorded it," she explains. She steps to one side. "Please, do come in. By all means. I'm sure he'll be pleased to see you, Mayor."

"Oh, there's no need for all that," he says as he steps over the threshold, shaking his umbrella off before collapsing it. "Just call me Hal."

"Okay . . . *Hal*. What about your friend?" she asks.

Hal looks back. Martin is in the driver's seat of the car, arms folded, watching the street. Hal leans in until his mouth is an inch from her ear. "Leave him be. He's a man of many talents—been working for me for years—but not very sociable, I'm afraid."

"I see," Mrs. Raxter says. She closes the door and leads him through the house to the basement. She stands at the top of the stairs and calls down. "You got a visitor up here, Gil. I'm sending him down."

Hal hears Gil shout back, "Huh?" but his wife doesn't bother responding. She tells Hal to go on down, make himself at home. Would he like a drink?

"Something cold, if you have it," he tells her. "If you don't, not to worry."

"I'm sure I can rustle something up," she says, blushing again.

Hal goes down the stairs. The basement is a good size. The bare brick walls have been painted white, there's durable carpet on the floor. Hal notes a pool table, a dart board, and two sofas situated in front of a pull-down screen. The game from last night is projected from the ceiling onto the screen. Gil sits watching it, dressed in a pair of shorts and a vest. He turns around to see who it is, and nearly leaps out of his seat.

"Morning," Hal says, smiling. Gil stands, his face startled, and Hal reaches over the sofa and shakes his hand. "It's been a long time."

"Sure has," Gil says, rescuing his hand from Hal's titanic grip.

Mrs. Raxter descends the stairs, carrying a glass of iced tea so cold the glass perspires. "Here you are, Mayor."

"Hal," he reminds her, taking the drink.

"Oh yes. Hal."

Hal watches her go back up the stairs, admiring her shapely bottom beneath her housedress—for a woman her age, she's in good shape. The door closes, giving them both privacy.

Gil swallows. "What the fuck are you doing here?"

Hal makes a face. "That's no way to greet an old buddy, is it? Where's your manners?"

"You're no buddy of mine, that's for sure," Gil spits.

Hal comes around the sofa, and Gil gets up. Hal takes a seat, then sips his drink. "Mmm, that's some good iced tea. Had us a cook when I was a boy. Made it just like that," he says, taking another sip. He regards the glass appreciatively. "Yeah, that's good. Especially in heat like we got now . . . though they say the weather's about to turn. Got some kind of storm front coming in. I say it's balmy out there. Wind and rain last night. Blue skies this morning. Balmy."

"What do you want?" Gil asks, still standing. "I told you years ago, I didn't want nothin' to do with you."

"I know you did."

"Then why're you here?"

Hal sets the glass down on a worn old coffee table in front of him. "Because we got business, you and I. And it can't wait."

"Business?" Gil asks, sitting on the other sofa, slowly, as if any sudden movements will provoke Hal to bare his fangs. "What're you talking about?"

Hal looks down, straightens his tie. "Any day now, IA is gonna come askin' you questions, Gil. About your involvement in certain things."

Gil shrugs. "So? I'm not in those files, and you know it. Same with our mutual friend."

"We all had a part to play."

"That's in the past."

"Not for some," Hal says, swallowing back the bitterness in his mouth. The distaste. "It's inevitable, Gil. It's why I need you to think carefully about what you say to them."

"What's that?" Gil watches as Hal reaches inside his jacket and produces a thick padded envelope. He hands it over and Gil counts what's inside. Looking up from the envelope, Gil says, "There's a lot of money here."

"There is."

"I take it you want my silence."

Hal nods slowly. "And your ignorance. You don't remember anything. You don't know names, locations, times. Nothing."

Gil folds the envelope over and hands it back to him. "I don't think I can do that."

Hal takes the envelope, disbelieving. "Really?"

"Really."

Hal shifts in his seat. "Did I ever tell you about old Roofy?"

"No. I do not believe you did," Gil says stiffly, his voice uncertain.

"That was our old dog. Just a mongrel, I suppose. Had fur that looked like old leather. You know the type?"

Gil nods.

"Beautiful animal. Had him from a pup. Well behaved. Never took a dump on the rug. That kind of pooch," Hal tells him. "Then one day, when he was about six years old, Roofy snatched my Daddy's paper and ran into the backyard with it. Daddy went out there, called Roofy back. He didn't come. So he walked over to the dog and reached out to get the paper back. D'you know what Roofy did?"

Gil doesn't say anything. Hal continues anyway, knowing he has a captive audience, knowing that the reason Gil hasn't said anything is because he's wondering where the story is going.

"Roofy dropped the paper and bit Daddy's hand. Hard enough to draw blood. What do you think Daddy did next, huh? I reckon you can imagine."

"Killed it?"

"Put it in the back of his car and drove it into town. Gave it to a local farmer. I never saw that dog again. You know what it taught me?"

"You're the one tellin' the story."

"It taught me, no matter how attached you get, you can't keep nothing around that's gonna turn on you. If there's any question of loyalty . . ."

Gil clears his throat. "I don't know why you're telling me this. The answer's no. I don't want any part in this. No more. I've had it covering for you. I got called in to help on all those cases. Helped you clean up. Did my part. But that was then. This is now. And the answer's no, Hal."

"You know," Hal says, shaking his head. "It's a real crying shame, Gil, old buddy."

"What is?"

"I loved my dog, but sometimes you need to have something you love taken away to learn hard lessons. I learned a hard lesson that day. It's a shame your kids mean so goddamn little to you," Hal says. "Of course, they're all older now. Flown the nest and all that. But just imagine how it might feel to lose one of them in some . . . unforeseen accident."

"Accident?" Gil says, eyes growing wide.

Hal nods slowly. "That's right. They're driving along, at full speed, and they hit the brakes only to find there's nothing there. It doesn't work. It'd be a tragedy."

Gil springs up. "Get out!"

"Now," Hal says, smiling, not budging an inch. "Don't be too hasty. You're a retired detective. You know the score. You know, all too well, these things happen. In almost every case, there's nothing anybody could have done to prevent them . . . unlike now."

Gil's hands tighten into fists at his sides. The blood rushes to his face. "I fuckin' swear, Hal, you son of a bitch, if you don't get out this house . . ."

"What? You'll strike the mayor?" Hal shakes his head. "You're smarter than that, Gil. Now sit down, calm down, don't take any of this personally. It's a business transaction. Think what you could do with that money. A nice vacation for you and the wife. Or a new car."

Gil slowly sits on the edge of the sofa, breathing fast, wanting to explode but knowing he can't.

"I saw that old station wagon out front. You're due a new vehicle. I know Ricky down at the showroom. I'm sure he'd give you a good price. Call it a friend's discount," Hal says, handing back the envelope of money. For a moment, it looks as though Gil will stick to his guns. But then he sags, snatches the packet from Hal's hands.

"There. I took your money. I'll keep my mouth shut," Gil says. "But don't think I don't regret what we did. Don't for a minute think that I'll forgive you for involving us in your dirty work. Marshall and me. We didn't have a choice."

"Funny thing is, there's always a choice," Hal says.

Gil glares at him. "Get the fuck out of my house." Hal stands, nods, then walks to the bottom of the stairs. Halfway up, Gil says, "Hey."

Hal stops. "Yeah, Gil? Got something you want to add?"

"Yeah, I reckon I do," Gil says. "If you ever knock on my door again, Hal, you'd better be wearing your piece. 'Cause I swear to God, I will plug you full of holes and happily do the time."

"Of that I have no doubt." The moment stretches out. "Pleasure seein' you again, Gil," Hal says finally. The smile drops, and all of a sudden the space separating the two men doesn't seem far enough. Hal's eyes bore into him, his demeanor completely changed. "Just you think about old Roofy. I don't know what I'd have done in my daddy's shoes. When something you trust turns on you like that, what choice do you have? I think that maybe I'd do the exact same thing. I mean, an untrustworthy servant is a miserable creature, wouldn't you agree?"

Gil swallows.

"Anyway!" Hal says, clapping his hands together. "See you around, old buddy. You take care now."

In the kitchen, Mrs. Raxter has her back to him, rinsing plates in the sink.

Hal closes the door to the basement behind him. "I'll be off now, Mrs. Raxter. Thank you kindly for the iced tea."

"Oh! Okay. Let me walk you out," she says.

Hal follows her to the front door, watching the sway of her hips.

"Well, thanks for stopping by," she says, opening the door for him.

Hal reaches into his pocket for his wallet. Produces one of his business cards and hands it to her. "Thought you might like to have this. That's my personal cell there, below my office number. And, of course, you know where I work."

Again, she blushes, looking down at the card, not sure what to do with herself. "Thank you . . . I'll keep it safe."

"Be sure you do," Hal says, reaching out, taking her hand in his. Ever so softly, ever so gently. She looks up into his face, and Hal sees the firecracker she must have been when Gil first married her. The girlish look in her eyes. He glances down the hall. The basement door is still closed.

Hal leans in, close to her ear. "I'm a busy man, but I always make the time for good, honest people such as yourself. Especially when they're so damned pretty."

He pecks her on the cheek, then leaves, smiling to himself as he opens his umbrella.

24

Turner Street is empty, as is the Hope and Ruin Coffee Bar.

Albie spots Harper right away. "You look like hell."

"Thanks," she tells him as he sits down across from her. "I took the liberty of ordering you a latte."

They have a window seat. It's quiet in there, no one sitting nearby who can snoop on their conversation.

"You're not frightened to be out in the open like this?" Albie asks.

"Strangely, no," Harper says. "This whole dodging bullets thing, it's becoming a habit."

"You're taking it better than I would. I'd be in hiding."

"Honestly, there *is* no way to take it. No rule book. I can only do what I'm doing. It's all I know." Harper pats her weapon. "Anyway, if they do try something on me again, I'm prepared."

"Amen," Albie says, lifting the side of his suit jacket to reveal his own holster. "Anyway, where were you last night? I thought you'd stay with us another night. I tried calling you, but . . ."

"I, uh, went to the station. Then I went back to my apartment."

"You did *what*?" Albie gasps. "Have you even slept?"

"Couple of hours." Harper lifts her coffee. "That's why me and Mr. Caffeine here are getting reacquainted with one another."

Albie is shocked. "Freehan doesn't want you there, Harper! What if she found out?"

"To be honest, I don't care if she does."

"So what did you find?" Albie asks.

"The mayor."

Albie frowns. "Hal Crenna?"

"One and the same."

"I knew his name appeared in the files Claymore kept . . . but surely he was questioned by Internal Affairs. Even the news of the cover-up that came out before the election didn't seem to make an impact. I figured he was off the hook."

"Hal Crenna, Lloyd Claymore, and Bill Marshall—their three names appear in the files of every one of Lester's victims. Admittedly, Claymore did his part in keeping a record of the truth, in the hope that one day the killer would be found . . . but regardless of that, those three men were happy to see the crimes covered up."

"Claymore is dead. And now Marshall is, too." He drinks some of his latte. Wipes the foam off his top lip.

"And so is the coroner who signed off on the falsified evidence—natural causes. Which leaves our beloved mayor."

Albie frowns. "You think Mayor Crenna is the next target?"

"I think Crenna killed Marshall and Morelli."

"Jesus." Albie's eyes go wide. "Why?"

"Think about it," Harper says. "Why would Crenna cover up Lester's murders? He was the senior detective on those cases. I've never bought into that notion that concealing the murders was about protecting tourism. You've seen Crenna's campaign posters around town, his endless press conferences. The guy is the definition of ambition. Wouldn't it have been better for his career if he'd found the killer and stopped him? Hauled Lester in and accepted the praise? So what was he really hiding?"

She allows Albie to absorb all of this in stunned silence for a few minutes. She knows it's a leap, and she doesn't have the most important answer yet either—why Crenna covered for Lester.

"Where are you and Ramirez at?" she says eventually.

"We checked a guy out yesterday. Ramirez was sure he'd be holding a grudge against Morelli."

"And?"

"Dead end," Albie says, glum. "Guy did his time, came out, and got himself back on track. Just didn't get that vibe from him, you know?"

"Yeah. I do. What about Ramirez? What did he think?"

"Same as me. He's back at the station; Freehan still has everyone looking into Morelli's and Marshall's old case files to see if anyone else had a grudge."

"Well, there's no need. The focus needs to be on the mayor."

"I agree. But, Harper, Freehan seems convinced Morelli was corrupt. And didn't she say Crenna was the one who brought her in?"

Harper goes to speak again, looks past Albie at a news crew assembling outside the Hope and Ruin.

Albie lowers his coffee, turns in his chair to see what she's looking at. The redheaded reporter from before is positioning herself in front of the glass just so. The cameraman adjusting his position, probably so that he can include the reporter and have Harper and Albie in the background, drinking their coffee as if they don't have another care in the world.

Harper shoots up from the table. "Son of a bitch," she says, heading for the door.

"Oh God," Albie says, taking after her.

Harper charges out front and gets in the reporter's face. "Are you kidding me? It's not enough you come to my home, and hound me there. But you're following me around town now?"

"We happened to be passing—"

Harper turns to the cameraman, knocks the camera to one side. He trains it back on her, unfazed.

"Please, don't touch the equipment," the reporter says. "Now, Detective, I was wondering if you could offer anything with regards to the ongoing investigation. Your apartment was shot at in the middle of the night, was it not?"

"None of your damned business. Now get the hell out of here."

"Why are you being targeted by gunmen, Detective?"

Harper jabs her with a finger. "I'm warning you. Before I ruin your day like you're ruining mine."

"Really, Detective? You're threatening a member of the press? What exactly are you going to do?"

Harper looks surprised. "Try this on for size."

Albie is in the doorway. "Harper, no!"

She doesn't hear him. Snatches the camera out of the cameraman's hands and smashes it on the ground. The reporter looks on in disbelief. "We'll be filing charges for this."

Harper goes back inside the coffee bar, pushing past Albie to escape the spectators outside. She stands with her hands on the front counter, breathing heavily.

"I can't believe you just did that," Albie says, shaking his head.

Harper turns around. "Most satisfying moment all week."

25

"The mayor will see you now," the secretary says, escorting Ida to the door.

Ida tries to remember to breathe. The secretary knocks, then holds the door open for her. The mayor of Hope's Peak rounds his desk to greet her. Practically crushes her hand with his big, strong, warm grip. The brilliance of his white teeth stands in stark contrast to the deep orange of his skin.

"Come in, come in," he says, showing her to one of a pair of chairs in front of his huge desk. "Please. Sit."

Ida sits down. The secretary closes the door, leaving them to talk privately. Hal seats himself on the other side of his desk. He smiles—his lips lift, mouth parting enough to show those white crocodile teeth.

Look into my eyes, my dear, and let me take a bite . . .

"Now, as you can imagine, I have much to do, and not enough hours in the day to do it," Crenna says. "But I'm glad you came by, Miss Partman, is it?"

"Partman. That's right."

His smile falters, just for a microsecond. Like a blip in a TV transmission. One of those blink-and-you'll-miss-it moments. Something about the name sounds familiar, but Ida can see he can't quite place it. At least not yet.

"You've had this appointment booked for several weeks now. I'm so sorry I couldn't get to you sooner. But as I said—"

"Not enough hours in the day," Ida finishes for him.

Breathe. Keep breathing.

His smile disappears completely. "Yes. So . . . how can I help you?"

"First things first, Mayor," Ida says, finding her grit. She feels shaky with nerves. The day she has thought about for months is finally here. She is confronting the man who allowed Lester to kill. He's as good as a murderer himself. If not worse. "My name ain't Partman. It's Lane. Ida Lane."

Crenna doesn't move an inch.

Ida smiles. "That name should ring a bell for you. Since it was my mother, Ruby, your brother killed."

"I don't know what you're talking about."

Ida scoffs. "Don't play coy with me, Mayor. I know all about it. What was it you told Lester? That you ain't got nothin' against culling a few niggers? Remember that one?"

Crenna's orange face is turning a decidedly crimson hue. "You're out of your mind, lady," he says, getting up. "I'm a respectable businessman. An upstanding, proud member of this humble community."

Ida looks him up and down. "You're a fucking liar is what you are."

Crenna grins. Walks around the desk to fix himself a drink. She watches as he pours scotch into a glass, then drops in two ice cubes picked from a covered bucket with a pair of black tongs.

"Now, now, there's no need for language such as that in this office. I sense a lot of anger. A lot of confusion."

Ida shakes her head. "No, Mayor. My head's never been clearer."

He takes a sip. Laughs at her. "Yeah?"

"I'm gonna see to it everyone in this town knows you were Lester's half brother. They'll see through your perfect hair and that fake-ass smile you got goin' on," Ida tells him.

Crenna sits back down behind his desk. "No."

"No?"

He smiles. "That's right. No. It's not the way this is going to play out, and I'll tell you why. I do remember you. At least . . . I remember your name. That little girl who fainted at her mama's funeral," he says, his eyes burrowing into her. "That same little girl who got sent to the mental hospital because she lost her fucking mind."

Ida starts shaking her head. "You can't get at me like this. You can't."

"Oh, but I think I can. I also think that I can get you committed, Miss Lane. Committed for a very long, miserable time," Crenna says. "You'll not get out this time. D'you hear me, you little bitch? Am I getting through?"

Ida doesn't know what to say. The confidence that brought her in here—that allowed her to talk to Crenna the way she has—dissipates like smoke.

The mayor lifts the glass to his mouth. Holds it there, relishing the moment. "You could say I get to complete my brother's work. He killed your mom . . . now I get to kill you. You'll die in there."

Ida can't maintain eye contact. Crenna sips his scotch, looking amused.

"You're a monster," Ida says, looking away. Shrinking into herself. *What made me think I could come here and do this? What have I done?*

"You'll *rot* in there." The mayor leans forward. *"ROT."*

Ida looks up. Glares at him. Feels the fire in her belly. In her chest. In her heart.

She stands up.

"When Jane Harper catches you, your family name won't be worth shit, Mayor. The people of this town will see you're no better than white trash and erase you from its memory. One day, they'll know what you really are. A dirty motherfucker!"

The mayor slams his fist down, scotch leaping from the glass and spilling across the desk. He gets up, chair falling back and heads for the door. "Get out! I'm calling security. They'll throw your ass out of here," he says, thundering down the corridor, yelling at the top of his lungs.

Ida fishes a plastic freezer bag out of her pocket and uses it to upend the glass over the desk—the last dregs of scotch left in the glass just adding to the mess that's already there. She inverts the bag so that her hand never touches it, then seals it. Ida just manages to get the glass in her jacket pocket before the mayor reappears in the doorway.

"Security is on its way."

"No need, I'm going," Ida tells him. As she tries to pass Crenna, he slams an arm out in front of her, stopping her in her tracks. He's close, his mouth mere inches away from her. Looking into his eyes, Ida can see the malice. Even if the glass she stole doesn't prove a genetic link between Crenna and Lester Simmons, she sees it there. An inherent darkness. She knows it is there. She has seen it. *Felt it.*

"I've devoted my life to this fucking place, to keep it the way it is. Keep it pure and innocent. I won't have my good name tarnished by the likes of you, understand?"

"You're deluded," Ida says, wanting ever so much to get away from him, his overwhelming aftershave and sour whiskey breath.

Crenna moves his arm. Two security guards intercept her, but she pushes through them.

As she walks briskly away, heading for the exit, she hears Crenna say, "Don't worry about her, boys. She's gonna be going away for a long, long time very soon."

They stand under the entrance of the coffee bar, sheltering themselves. Cold rain blasts Main Street, a strong wind driving it over the blacktop in torrents. The buildings around them creak and moan.

Albie shifts on his feet. "So what we've been discussing . . . Do we take it to Freehan?"

Harper scoffs. "Are you nuts? She'd never buy it."

"She doesn't seem completely unreasonable."

"Really? If we turn up with no evidence, nothing to support what we're saying, she'll laugh in our faces," Harper tells him.

"Wait a second," Albie says, digging into his pocket. He looks at his cell phone, eyes wide. "Oh Christ, Harper."

"What is it?"

He shows her the screen: INCOMING CALL—FREEHAN.

"Want me to answer it for you?" Harper offers. "I'm in the mood for a battle."

"Hell no, I do not," he says, picking up the call and walking off to speak with the captain.

Harper opens her umbrella, looks across the street, sees a familiar truck making a U-turn to swing around to her side. It screeches to a halt. The door springs opens.

"Ida?"

"Sugar! Thought I'd find you here," she says. "Get in. I got somethin'."

"What?" Harper says, striding toward the open passenger door of the truck. She climbs in, slams the door shut.

Ida's short, tight curls are beaded with raindrops, as is her jacket. It only just started raining, which means Ida hasn't been in the truck long. And she's worked up over something.

"Ida, talk to me. You look upset."

"Upset? You don't know the half of it."

Harper studies her. "What's happened? This isn't like you . . ."

Ida shakes her head, "No, it ain't. I've lost my mind."

"Talk to me."

"I went and saw the mayor."

That throws her. Harper frowns. "The mayor? Hal Crenna? Why?"

"Yeah. I had to. Ever since . . . well, you know . . . since everything that happened with Lester Simmons, those girls, I've known it would come. And today it did. I got in there and faced up to him."

"Slow down, Ida," Harper says, struggling to keep up. Ida is babbling. Her eyes darting this way and that with feverish energy. "Why did you go see Hal Crenna?"

"Because I had to, sugar. I had to go see that man. Tell him what he is."

"Go on."

Ida looks at her, eyes swimming. "When I touched Lester Simmons, I saw something. And I kept it from you all this time. Didn't tell you nothin' about it."

"What did you see?" Harper asks. "Talk to me."

Ida bites her bottom lip. Orders her thoughts before speaking again. "I saw Lester open the front door to a man claimin' he was his brother."

It sinks in.

Harper sits back. Awful realization washing over her like nausea. "No."

"Yes, Jane. The mayor of Hope's Peak is Lester Simmons's half brother. I saw it. He told Lester himself. Said he'd look out for him. Crenna senior had an affair with Lester's mom."

"So that's why . . . ," Harper says. She looks out the window. Rain falls more heavily now. "And you confronted the mayor about this?"

"Sure did. It felt frightening, and crazy. But it felt good, too."

"Are you an idiot, Ida?" Harper snaps, glaring at her. "What were you thinking? You should have told me about this."

"I know. I—"

"No!" Harper slams her hand down on the dashboard. "Damn it, Ida! You've got yourself in a lot of trouble. Instead of bringing this to me. Trusting me. Instead of doing *that*, you went solo. Put yourself right in harm's way."

Ida can't match, or hold, Harper's fierce gaze. "I know. I'm sorry. So, so sorry."

Harper breathes. Tries to calm down.

She reaches out, places a hand on Ida's shoulder. "Don't be sorry. Be smart. You're sure that it was Crenna in your vision?"

"Oh, sugar, I've never been more certain of anything," Ida says.

"Okay," Harper says. "Okay." It explained Crenna's involvement. Why he was all over those files, right at the heart of the cover-up. But convincing IA was going to be a different matter. Convincing Freehan . . .

"I was going to tell you, but then I got it stuck in my head. I don't do anger, Jane. Not really. But when I saw him parading himself about, like he'd never done anybody a day's harm in his entire life . . . I don't know. It was like somethin' just went and snapped inside me."

"Well, you're telling me now," Harper says. "We can sort this out. I can investigate him directly, see what dirt I can dig up. But I need to prove that he was Lester's relation. If I tell Freehan you told me—as much as I believe you—she won't buy it without something tangible to convince her."

Ida reaches down, produces a ziplock bag with a drinking glass in it. She holds it up by the corner.

"I might save you some trouble."

Harper points at it. "What the hell is it?"

"The glass he was drinking from when we had our meeting. Got his DNA all over it, I reckon," Ida says. She hands it over. "It's gotta be something, right?"

"Ida, I can't accept this. It's not evidence."

"Of course it is, sugar. I got it for you right there," Ida says.

Harper holds the bag. "Sure, we can run it for a match, see what happens . . . but it can't be used against him; it's stolen property, there's no chain of evidence."

Ida runs her hands over her face. Massages her forehead, groaning.

"Look, I'll pass it on. And if it does come back that he's Lester's brother—"

"He is," Ida interjects.

Harper nods. Looks out the window at Albie, ending his call. "Listen, I'd better go. Will you go straight home? By the looks of you, you've had quite a day."

"Yeah," Ida says. "I will. Don't worry 'bout me." Harper goes to leave the truck, and Ida reaches across, grabs her wrist. "Jane. Wait."

Harper's eyes move from Ida's hand on her wrist to Ida's face.

She lets go.

"Ida, we're fine. I promise. I may not understand why you kept this a secret, but I respect it," Harper says. "I respect you."

Ida smiles softly. "Thank you, sugar."

"Now get home." Harper shuts the door and walks away.

Albie puts his cell phone away, making a face because he's getting wet.

"What did she say?" Harper asks. She moves aside to let Albie under the umbrella with her.

Albie wipes water from his brow. "She wants me at the station ASAP."

Harper frowns. "Really? What the hell for?"

"That camera you broke? That you yanked out of the guy's hand and smashed on the ground? Well, it's all over the local news. The whole incident."

"Wait a second. How can I be over the news if I broke the camera?" Harper asks.

They hurry to Harper's car. She glances back to see Ida's truck joining the traffic.

"Look, that's not important, Harper," Albie says. "Jesus."

"I thought this place had one news channel."

"It does."

Harper shakes her head. "I swear, sometimes this town doesn't make any logical sense."

"Anyway, what is *that* in the bag?"

Harper lifts it up for him to see. "This?"

"Yeah."

"*This* is a drinking glass, with a dribble of scotch left in it. *This* is evidence."

"Evidence?"

Harper unlocks the car. "Yes."

"I'm sorry, I'm not following. Evidence?"

"Just get in," Harper says with a roll of her eyes. "I'll explain on the way."

26

Rain beats down hard, wipers squeaking as they work to clear the windshield.

"Is that her?" Albie asks as Harper pulls into the parking lot at the front of the station.

"Who?"

Albie nods in the direction of the entrance. Standing beneath the shelter with her arms folded is Captain Freehan, mouth pinched tight as a cat's ass.

"God, she's waiting for us," Albie mumbles.

Harper shakes her head. "Speak up. She can't hear you from all the way over there. She's a hard-ass, but she's not omnipotent."

"You don't know that."

"We had nothing to do with Ida going to see Crenna . . ."

Albie unclips his seat belt. "She told me I couldn't have anything to do with you. Ordered me to keep my distance. Here we are, arriving at the station together."

"After what Ida told us, there can't be any more half measures, Albie," Harper says. "If she says that she saw it in a vision, I believe her. That man is Lester's half brother."

"Yeah, and we both know what Freehan thinks of Ida's testimony."

Harper thumps his arm. "Hey, we have the glass Ida gave us. Okay? This could be what we need to make Freehan see sense. The DNA will be a match."

Albie looks worried. "In the meantime, she knows we've been working together."

"I'll take the blame. Come on."

The rainwater cascades down either side of the shelter covering the entrance. Freehan scowls at them. They both get out of the car, run through the rain to the front of the building.

"Right on cue," Freehan tells them, her face stern. "Two assholes for the price of one."

"Bit harsh, isn't it?" Harper says.

Freehan raises a finger. "You do not get to question me, Detective. After your fracas with the press and the stunt your friend pulled with the mayor, you're lucky I'm not working with the union to negotiate the terms of your permanent departure."

"I'm sure Ida had legitimate reasons for speaking to the mayor. We didn't know anything about it."

Freehan looks at Albie. *"We?"* she says, the word rolling on her tongue like a lozenge. "So this is a partnership, is it?"

"No, it's nothing like that," Harper says quickly. "I roped him into helping me out. If anyone is to blame, it's me."

"Don't try to protect him," Freehan fires back. "He can take what's coming, the same as you."

"What *is* coming?" Albie asks, uncertainly.

Freehan looks at them both. "You realize the shit you two are causing me? I've got the captain of this department shot down outside his home. I've got a well-known retired officer—liked by everyone, it seems to me—killed in the street, in full view of the public. Your place gets shot to bits late at night for no apparent reason. I didn't realize this place was the playground of Mexican street gangs."

Harper snorts. "I think I have a right to see this finished. I'm only trying to help."

"Well, you're not," she says, drawing a deep breath, her back straight, chest puffed out. "I'm sorry, Harper. I know your situation, but you are too corrosive to this investigation."

"Captain—"

"Besides, you're already on leave!"

Harper's hands ball into fists at her sides. "I don't care what you think about Ida's gift to see things the rest of us can't, but her abilities have been proven. She told us what she saw when she touched Lester Simmons's body."

"We have evidence linking him to Hal Crenna," Albie says.

"Evidence? What evidence?"

Albie hands the glass in the ziplock bag to Freehan.

She looks at it. "What's this?"

"It's got Crenna's DNA on it."

Freehan looks past him to Harper. "Seriously? Is *this* your evidence? How was it obtained?"

"Ida swiped it off his desk when she saw him," Harper explains. "I know we can't use it, officially, but it will prove that what she is saying is right. Hal Crenna is Lester Simmons's half brother."

"This is absurd. And you're right, even if it does come back . . . it's useless. In fact, you're breaking the law by having it in your possession."

Harper says, "Lester Simmons was the product of a liaison between his mother and Hal Crenna's father. I believe the mayor knows this, and has been covering for his half brother all this time."

"Do you know how far-fetched that sounds? You're making some pretty big leaps here, Detective," Freehan says. "You really think *the mayor* was covering up the actions of a serial killer and arranged the murder of two colleagues just to help out his *half brother*? I can appreciate that you're making connections. But I am not about to go *accusing* the mayor of this town of being involved in anything at this time."

"He wasn't the mayor then. He was the captain. Who else could have directed the cover-up, ensured the silence of all those other officers? Besides, if he thought that either Morelli or Marshall had an inkling that he was related to Lester Simmons . . . it makes sense that he would eliminate them."

"That's so far-fetched, I'm not even going to begin to take it seriously." Freehan turns to Albie. "As for you, I told you to steer clear of her, didn't I? You should've stuck a little closer to Ramirez. It would have made this a lot easier."

"Made . . . *what* easier?" Albie asks.

Freehan sighs. "I'm suspending you, Detective Goode. Effective immediately. Go home until I decide what to do with you."

Albie looks down at the ground. He doesn't say anything.

Shit. What have I done? Harper wonders, looking at her young protégé.

"As for you, please do me the favor of backing off," Freehan tells her. "I told you once; now I'm telling you again. The next time, I'll have you locked up. Let us find whoever is behind these shootings and restore the faith of this town in its PD."

"What about that evidence?" Harper asks her. "I can swallow you discrediting my work on the Lester Simmons case. I can take the personal attacks and the disrespect. But Stu gave his life to stop that killer. We did good work, regardless of what anyone else says."

"This?" Freehan holds the glass up to the light. The misting from Hal Crenna's lips visible on the rim. The captain looks across at Harper, and they lock eyes, just for a second. It's enough for Harper to see that, despite their differences, Morelli's replacement is just as dedicated to her job as her predecessor. She lowers her arm, the evidence bag clutched tightly in her hand.

She knows it. I can see it on her face. She can't outright dismiss this, despite the fact she probably should.

"Get out of here. The both of you," Freehan tells them. "More importantly, tell your mentally ill friend to stay the hell away from the goddamn mayor."

She walks away, and Harper is relieved to see her still carrying the bagged evidence. Hopefully within minutes Freehan will see to it that that glass is on its way to the lab for analysis.

"Are you okay?" Harper asks Albie.

He looks at her, face numb. She reaches out to rub his shoulder, but he shrugs her off.

"Albie . . . ," Harper says, uselessly, but he's already walking away. Before she knows it, all she can see is the back of him crossing the street. She watches him go, her heart sinking.

So young, so inexperienced. And she might have ended his career before it even had the chance to begin.

27

The boy cycled past the wood mill at the edge of town, glancing up at the sign over the front of the building—weathered now and in need of replacing. The same sign had hung over the entrance to the wood mill when his father was a boy.

It was late—the sun arced over the horizon, beneath a bank of thick white clouds. Overhead the sky grew darker. He was forever going past the wood mill, wondering if he was destined to one day own the same mill that established his family's name as an institution in Hope's Peak.

The boy focused on the road, eyes narrowed, legs pumping, venting a frustration that had set in with puberty. He'd nagged his mother into buying him the bike—a racing-car-red one he'd spotted in the window of Moreton & Son on his way home from school. For once, his father had backed him. Agreed he could have the bike, if only in the hope it would give him a chance to "work off some of that puppy fat."

It worked. Since getting it, he'd become lean. There were muscles in his legs, in his calves. His tummy had flattened out (though he was still fond of the sundaes Harriet, their cook, put together on Friday evenings). At eleven years old, there was a definite buzz from exercise. A sense of freedom he didn't get from anything else.

When he saw a car cut through the crossroad up ahead, it took a moment or two for him to realize it was his father's Lincoln. The boy broke course, turned to follow. A cool wind rushing up from somewhere, fanning out his T-shirt.

The car was in danger of leaving him for dust, but he gave the pedals his all, keeping pace with the Lincoln as it headed down a road bordered by swaying crops, yellowed with sun. His legs burned with the effort of keeping up with the car. He used the little headlight on the front of the handlebars to see. Up ahead, the Lincoln careened to the left, its taillights disappearing. The boy pedaled faster, took the same turn. A huge building emerged from the gloom like a black monolith against the dark sky. Dim illumination poured out from within, but there was nothing welcoming about the place.

He stopped and considered his options.

Turn around and go home. You're in trouble enough already.

His feet found the pedals, and he cycled toward the big old house, watching as his father walked through the front door, followed closely by his driver. The boy cycled around the side of the building, leaned his bike against the wall. Sounds came from inside—voices and cackling laughter. Heart beating fast in his chest, he walked around to the front of the building and placed his hands on the door, left ajar. Mustering all his courage, he pushed the door open, slipping silently inside.

The house had an enormous hall at its center, a wide staircase at one end, and a landing going all the way around the top. The place was run-down, abandoned. Walls crumbling, the whole place thick with damp. A busted pipe trickled water down one wall, eroding the plaster in the process.

The boy crept up the stairs, crawled along the top landing and looked down between the banisters. A dozen men in long white robes and tall white hoods surrounded a fire on the floor, ghostlike faces lit from below by the firelight, the holes in their hoods all the darker for it. They stood in a circle, conversing with one another in low, spidery voices. The skin prickled at the back of his neck.

"We already have one of them on that street. One is enough."

"These people are like flies."

"Did me some reading the other night. Do you know in the Civil War there was a church someplace? They stuffed it full of them and locked it from the outside. Then you know what they did? Burned that fuckin' church to the ground! Wish we could do something like that. Round 'em all up and get rid of them."

"Jesus, that's hard-core . . . even for you."

A jovial chuckle. "What? I'm serious—"

"Okay, let's settle down," a stern voice commanded. He knew that voice—his father's. "I gotta get back early tonight."

"Sure thing."

"And enough of that shit. Nobody's burning anyone. That's the sort of radical, psychotic behavior that's gonna put Hope's Peak on the map for all the wrong reasons. So, are we still debating what to do with that black family on Hudson Street?"

"Word is the big daddy has put in an offer on the old café. Now, I ain't got nothin' against having a few coloreds in town. It's good to have a few here and there, you know, for variety. I mean, ain't nobody gonna tell me crushed potatoes is any good without some black pepper. Amiright?"

"Amen."

"But we've got enough as it is. We're overrun. I'm not saying any of us here are opposed to the blacks' existence. I mean, they got their uses."

"Damn right."

His father spoke up again. "Last thing we need is them spooks serving their African foods here. I don't think our summer vacationers will appreciate curried goat, or whatever else these godforsaken people cook, served to 'em at the old café."

"I appreciate that. It doesn't fit the town. And the café should go to somebody local. But to keep up appearances, we've got to be seen as . . . inclusive. You know that. We all know that."

"Let's put it to vote, then," his father boomed over the chatter. "All those in agreement we should drive these spooks out of town?"

There was no need for a vote against it. The decision of the elders was unanimous.

The boy crawled backward, slowly, so as not to make a sound. He didn't want to turn his back on the men below in their white sheets, lit like devils by the firelight and fringed with darkness. At the end of the landing he stood up, turned around—

Found himself faced with the torso of a man. The man's hand clamped over his mouth before he could cry out. The man dragged him into the shadows, the boy's feet skidding uselessly along the dusty floorboards as he was taken to a room.

The door closed. "What the hell?"

His father's driver, Eli. The boy blinked up at him.

"If I take my hand away from your mouth, are you going to scream?"

The boy shook his head.

Eli removed his hand, hunkered down in front of him. "What are you doing here?"

"I followed you. On my bike."

Eli shook his head, a shadow crossing his worry-lined face. "This is serious. You shouldn't be here. If your daddy finds out . . ."

"He won't. If you let me go."

"Of course I'm lettin' you go . . . but I'm worried about you." Eli looked out through the open doorway, waved him over. "Head down that stairwell there. Don't stop."

"Okay."

"I want you to ride fast. Do you hear me?"

"Yes, sir."

Eli looked at him. "You're a good boy, Hal. You shouldn't have seen any of this. This ain't the place for you to be."

The boy didn't know what to say. Eli opened the door, hand at the small of the boy's back propelling him through the shadows. The boy flew down the stairs, running for the front door of the old house. Took his bike from the wall, hooked one foot into the pedal, then pushed himself away at top speed. *The boy rode hard for home. Halfway there he had to come off the road and hide behind a bush as his father's car hurtled past. Peering through the foliage, he thought he saw Eli look his way, but he couldn't be sure.*

He got home late, told his parents that he got caught up at his friend's house.

When his father passed him later in the hall on his way to bed, the boy could smell the smoke from the fire on him.

◆　◆　◆

Two days later, he rode through town and turned down Hudson Street. Saw a black family loading their belongings into the back of a station wagon. Two girls and their parents. The father glanced up as the boy cycled past—he had a split lip and a swollen eye—so swollen it was almost shut.

The man turned to look at the empty café—windows smashed, the inside burned out.

The clipped wings of somebody's dream.

There were other families like that one. And the town would stay the way it had always been . . . as long as there were men like Daddy to protect it.

28

The wipers struggle to push the water sheeting the windshield. Rain and wind forcing Ida to drive slow and steady as she heads home in the dark. Patti Smith comes on the radio, and Ida leans across the cab to turn it up, thinking of how Jane would like the song.

The road ahead is shiny black, the rain heavy and furious. Ida drives with both hands firmly on the wheel, fighting the wind. She watches as a small two-door zooms up from behind, then darts into the other lane to overtake her. Ida shakes her head.

Speed on much as you like. I'm not stepping on the gas for anybody. It always feels nuts to her when drivers risk their own safety just to get a little ahead. Better to cruise along as you are and be patient. Especially on back roads like this one where there are turns that prohibit the visibility of oncoming traffic. More so when you're driving at night in bad weather. Ida shudders to think what might have happened if anything had been heading the other way when that car passed her. She has seen enough death.

I can't believe I went to Crenna's office and confronted him today, Ida thinks. She is frightened, shook up . . . but at the same time, she feels light. As if a burden has been lifted—one she has been brooding over for months. Ever since she laid her hands on Lester Simmons and learned the terrible truth.

The mayor of Hope's Peak was his half brother. Covered for him. Kept him killing.

A flash of light erupts in the rearview. Another hustler trying to get somewhere fast, chasing her tail. He races up behind her showing no signs of stopping. The road is straight and continues like this for the next two miles. It's clear for the car behind to overtake her, but it doesn't.

Patti Smith's voice rises, a chant for the ages as potent as when it was first released. Ida glances in the rearview. "Damn fool. Why you just sittin' there?"

The car accelerates. Rams the back of her truck, metal screaming against metal. Ida is thrown against the wheel, no time to react. The car slams into her truck again, and the steering wheel slips from her palms.

The truck trembles, shudders, veers to the right. Dips down off the road, the front plowing through gathered water, causing it to explode like a geyser.

Ida squeezes her eyes shut. Hurtling down the pitch-black embankment, her truck hits something in the dark with an enormous squeal of wrenching metal, and she is pinned back in her seat.

The night turns over. Ida screams. Falling, tumbling, engine roaring, hitting the sodden ground. The truck flips over, crashing down on its roof as it comes to rest on the ground.

Ida opens her eyes. She is upside down, the radio playing. Patti Smith still wailing. Ida finds the seat belt release, pushes it down, falls forward. Gasping, it takes all her strength to twist around and attempt to open the door. The rain pummels the underbody of the truck like an onslaught of ball bearings. In the darkness, a single beam of light falls upon the side of the cab as someone makes their way down the embankment.

Help, Ida thinks. *Please be help.*

Her mind a fog of emotions, unsure what has happened, Ida knows she needs to get out of the truck. She tries the door. It won't open.

The light draws closer. *What if it's whoever ran me off the road? What if they're coming down here to finish the job?*

Ida scoots over to the passenger's side of the cab and yanks the door handle.

It opens a few inches.

A man appears, his straining face half lit from the flashlight in his hand. He pulls on the passenger's side door, the edge of it catching in the dirt. Ida squints against the glare in her eyes, wondering if she should shrink back, if she should fight him off. She can't see his face, just jeans and a rugby top. Boots smothered in slimy mud.

The door grates as the man forces it to yield. His hands are in the cab, and now Ida can see his face—a thug of a man, dripping wet. Wet gray hair, scars on his face, and a mean glint in his eyes.

He's not here to help.

The engine dies, and Patti Smith falls silent.

He reaches in for her. Ida hits out, screeching, not sure of herself—or what she's doing. He grabs at her shirt, pulls her toward him like a troll snaring a hobbit from a cave.

"Help!" Ida screams, finding her voice. "Help me!"

The man pulls her out, throws her down on the mud, the breath knocked out of her. Rain falls hard from the unrelenting black sky. Ida pushes herself up to her knees, then to a sitting position, dazed. Her attacker walks in front of her, boots sloshing on the sodden ground.

Ida looks up. "Please don't hurt me."

"Sorry, luv," he says, slamming his fist into her face. The night busts open, an explosion of stars, hurt, and brain sparkle. Ida moans. Hears herself sobbing from afar, as if someone else is making those noises.

He drags her up the incline, toward the road, her legs flailing uselessly behind her in the muddy earth, feet little more than deadweights. At the top, the man maneuvers her into the back of his car. Ida cries out, tries to push back against him, but he's too strong. Before she can make another sound, he silences her with a length of duct tape across her mouth. He wraps the tape around her ankles to stop her kicking.

Hopelessness sets in—hopeless that help will come, hopeless that she will be out of pain and discomfort anytime soon, hopeless that she will ever get to collect the keys for that new apartment in Hope's Peak.

Lightning strikes in the distance, filling the sky with thin white light. The man takes her wrists, holds them together as he winds tape around them. Ida feels a jolt from his skin touching hers. Sometimes the connection can't be helped. It's made without her, like the separate fields of two magnets interacting.

Ida sees the man waiting for Morelli to turn around before shooting him in the chest. Watching Morelli's shocked expression, then firing again, hitting the captain in the neck.

Going to Harper's apartment late at night. Thunder and lightning detonating around him as he fires at the windows, the walls, then ran when Harper gave chase.

Martin clamping his foot down on the accelerator and ramming the back of her truck, seeing it swerve, then pitch over the side of the road, rolling until it crashes to a stop at the bottom.

Ida sees her captor dressed in fatigues, holding a service rifle. He walks toward an injured Iraqi soldier. The soldier holds up his hands, blood in his mouth, eyes filled with fear, begging for mercy in his mother tongue—terror has its own universal language. Ida watches as Martin grins, points his rifle at the Iraqi, and fires into him again and again and again.

Ida sees him directing some men to dig a hole in a field. Slapping a hysterical young woman in the mouth, the sound from his open palm striking the side of her face ringing out like the snap of a leather belt.

Yelling, "Shut your fucking mouth!" at her in a British accent.

She sees Martin at home, on his own, watching the television with a cigarette in one hand and an open bottle of vodka in the other. Lifting it to his lips to drink without bothering to pour it into a glass. His apartment is dark save for the flickering, ethereal blue light of the television.

The connection is broken—he's let go of her, throwing her back onto the seat, unaware of what he has shared with her. But the residuals are still in her mind, though fading fast.

He walks into a house, hands a woman an envelope of money. "He said to expect the same every month. Cash only, so don't ask for it any other way."

"What if I want to take him to court?"

The man looks across the room at a sleeping baby in a crib. "Then that child will grow up without a mother. You think on that."

Dissipating like smoke now, she sees him sitting at a kitchen table, a gun in his hand. He is crying, holding his head in his hands, a picture of misery under the stark kitchen light hanging over his head. He is his own judge, jury, and executioner. One day he will take the plunge, lift the gun, and tap his temple. It's just a matter of when. But what's important is that the potential of that outcome is inside of him.

In fact, it's inevitable.

Ida opens her eyes. The connection is completely gone now, but what is left is a lasting impression of a man who is happiest when he is causing hurt to others. A man who delights in mayhem and is restless when left to his own devices.

The car is moving. Mouth swollen and throbbing, her whole face feels like it's been pounded by a hammer. She closes her eyes, tries to order her thoughts. Ida searches deep down for the strength to be brave . . . but that strength is hard to find.

◆　◆　◆

Harper's cell vibrates in her bag.

She yanks it out, answers it just in time. "Harper."

"Hey, this is Officer Weinberg."

It takes a moment for the penny to drop. Weinberg and Tasker were the attending officers when Harper and Stu were called to the scene of Lester's last victim, Gertie. "Hey, how are you?"

"Uh . . . ," he says.

"What is it?"

"I've got some bad news. I'm at the roadside, just outside Chalmer. We've found a truck. Looks like it was in some kind of collision. Ran straight off the side of the road and tipped over. There's a huge dent in the passenger's-side door."

Harper frowns. "Did you say *truck*?"

"That's why I'm calling. We all know the two of you worked together, and as far as we can tell, she has no next of kin. I thought you should know right away," Weinberg says.

"Wait, wait, wait," Harper says, one hand against her head as it threatens to burst. "Are you saying that's Ida Lane's truck?"

"Sorry, I thought I said that already," Weinberg says. "Plate checks out. I've run it through the system. Definitely hers."

"Jesus . . ."

"Hey. There's something else."

She closes her eyes. Sits on the edge of her sofa, legs turned to jelly. Already she pictures the scene of the accident. Truck upside down, Ida's limp arm hanging from the open car door.

"Give it to me," Harper says. "She's gone, isn't she?"

"Yeah, we've looked everywhere, and we can't find her. There are some trees about fifty feet away, so we're about to go looking in there. But by the look of things, she got out the truck and walked on up to the road. At least, that's how it looks from the footprints. I mean, the water's collecting down there around the truck. It's almost impossible to get down there from the road. We had a helluva time."

Harper takes a deep breath. No Ida is good news.

There have only been a few times in her life that she has felt everything hurtling about her in a blur: recovering from The Moth's attempt at strangling her to death; her father telling her he was dying, that he wanted to see her one last time; her husband telling her their marriage was over at the Saint Francis Memorial Hospital back in San Francisco; shooting Lester Simmons dead; the first time she and Stu made love.

What surfaces like a buoy in a turbulent sea is her memory of Ida reading a dead body for the first time. Air humming with static, the sense that she was seeing something truly remarkable and frightening at the same time.

"Detective Harper? Are you there?"

She comes to. "Yes. Yes, I'm here. So there's no body?"

"No body, just footprints. Two sets."

Harper swallows. "Two?"

"Yes. Could be the car that collided with her, maybe," Weinberg says. "I mean, I'm not an expert or anything. Obviously. Do you want me to call you back once I know anything?"

Harper tells him yes and ends the call. She sits in the quiet stillness of her apartment, numb, unsure what to do next. Caught in the mental fog that has descended.

Thunder growls outside. Harper checks her weapon, grabs her keys, and heads for the door.

Into the storm.

29

The Simmons house has metal shutters on the windows and the doors. It is in a far worse state than the last time Ida was here. Much of the house's exterior has been battered—pelted by bricks, stones, and whatever else the youth of Hope's Peak can get their hands on. A can of black paint has been thrown against the house, leaving half of a Rorschach inkblot where it has splashed up one corner.

Martin reaches through the door into the back seat, the storm threatening to blow him over. Ida has had time to calm down, to think through her situation. Her truck will be found. Forensics will discover that she was pulled from the wreckage. Jane will be on her way.

But how will she know where I am? She can't know that I've been brought here. No way.

Ida knows to think that way is to admit defeat already. Throughout the car journey, she had worked at the tape binding her ankles. It wasn't as tight as her captor had thought it was. Now it is slack. Her mind races as Martin carries her in his arms toward the house, grunting from the effort.

I may only get one shot, she thinks as she works one foot free of the tape that held her ankles together.

Martin almost loses his footing on the sodden path, the rain hammering them on all sides, sharp and cold, stinging like grit. She has no choice but to bury her face against him to shield it. He takes her around the side of the building, and Ida feels a chill in her bones.

Here he lived.

Here he died.

There are the same metal shutters over the windows and back door, but one noticeable difference: the one over the back door has been unlocked, and stands open. Inside there is only darkness. Ida glances about. A garden, a shed, old trash cans, a swing. It fills her heart with dread—this place, where Lester did his work, where he lived with his madness, his obsession.

My mother was his obsession.

Martin crosses the threshold of the back door. Thunder explodes around them, and he falters.

Ida tenses.

His grip loosens.

Now.

She kicks out, causing him to stumble back. Ida bucks herself out of his arms, and he drops her on the wet ground. She scrambles away from him in the pitch black, not knowing where she should go. But knowing she should get away from the house. Kicking herself away from him as best she can with bound feet and hands.

Martin pounces on her, pushing her down to the ground. Face in the dirty rainwater, Ida cries out. He hauls her to her feet, big fingers biting into her so hard, they draw blood. He steers her toward the open doorway, the dark innards of the house awaiting her like the maw of hell.

"You ain't going nowhere," he snarls, shoving her forward. Her eyes dart left and right, and she resists the urge to be sick—the impulse to give up. Acid rises in the back of her throat. They walk through the kitchen, and Martin slams the door behind them. Blocking out the storm, the howl of the wind, the incessant rumble of thunder. "Through there."

Ida finds herself in the hallway. It all comes flooding back. The spot where Jane lay, lifting her gun to shoot Lester. Where Stu was hacked to death with an axe. Her eyes fall to where Lester bled out, breathing his last. She pressed her hands against him and saw his journey to the other side. His descent into oblivion.

Ida comes to a standstill, an influx of memories and emotions rushing back. Martin shoves her from behind. "Keep going."

Ida walks past the stairs, looks up. A lightning strike nearby suddenly illuminates the inside of the house. Her heart skips a beat. At the top of the stairs is Lester—the pillowcase over his head, belt around his neck, staring back at her through misshapen black eyeholes. The white cotton material sucking in and out with each breath. Axe dangling at his side. Blood splattered up his bare torso.

The flash fades and so does he. Ida can't tear her eyes away. Martin grabs her by the arm and drags her through to the living room. A gas camping lantern sits on a table, casting dim, sulfuric light that does little to illuminate such a dingy, oppressive room.

The mayor of Hope's Peak is sitting with one side of his face lit by the lantern, the other obscured by shadow. Martin drops her onto a fabric sofa. Damp, stinking of mold and age.

"Any trouble?" Hal asks.

"Tried getting away," Martin tells him, glaring at Ida as he talks. "Look at the state of me."

Hal looks down at Martin's jeans. They're covered in mud. "Apart from that?"

"Those old Volvos are built like tanks. I knew it would take her out. Ran her straight off the road. Should've seen that truck roll, Hal. Like something outta a movie."

Crenna gets to his feet. Standing in front of the lamp, the mayor looms over her like a specter. "Well, well, well."

Martin rips the tape off Ida's mouth. The pain sears her skin, leaves it burning.

Hal grins. "That's better."

Martin dries his face with an old rag. Works his fingers through his dripping wet hair, then stands with his back against the wall. There's a cut on his elbow. Blood dripping onto the floor.

"Watch the outside," Hal tells him. "We don't want any interruptions."

Martin nods silently and leaves the room.

"You're crazy," Ida says, looking up at Hal. Voice weak. "He nearly killed me. I'm lucky to be alive after that crash."

"Marty is very skilled," Hal tells her, bypassing the fact that she could have been killed when her truck was run off the road. "He knows what he's doing."

"Knows how to hurt people, you mean."

"We both do."

Hal smiles. Lowers himself back onto the old wooden chair next to the lamp, hands clasped between his knees.

He looks so out of place dressed to the nines in this tumbledown relic of a house, hair swept back over his head, oily skin clementine orange.

"We all know how to hurt people, Miss Lane. Take you, for instance. The hurt you've caused this town. Empowering Detective Harper's belief that there's some kind of . . ." He waves one hand, fishing for the word. Clicks his fingers. "Conspiracy."

Ida is baffled by the connections the mayor is making—and what his assumptions might mean for her chances of leaving this house in one piece. "Any conclusions Jane came to, she came to on her own."

Hal reaches inside his suit jacket and produces a folded paper. "This is her report on what went down here the night of Lester Simmons's death. Seems you're more involved than I first thought."

Ida swallows. *This guy is cuckoo.*

He holds up the sheet of paper, crumpling it into a ball as his hand becomes a fist.

"I don't pretend to understand what it is you do. But what I do know is that you helped Detective Harper create this whole convoluted story about cover-ups and corruption that, frankly, doesn't exist. All of it extrapolated from . . . what? Old files? Your psychic fucking visions? Give me a break."

"I don't know what you're talking about," Ida says.

"You've made her see what isn't there," Hal says.

Ida shakes her head. "I can't influence anybody. That's not who I am."

"You're some kind of . . ." He clicks his fingers again, searching for the word. *"Psychic."*

Ida says, "I helped Jane catch that killer. I helped her stop your brother."

Something changes in the mayor. His eyes are dark, face slack at the mention of Lester. It didn't so much touch a nerve as sucker punch him in the gut.

"I was able to see him through his victims' eyes," Ida continues, rambling now, feeling desperate, the sweat trickling down the back of her neck. Thunder booms around the house, wind shaking the house all around them, riding a meteorological fault line. "See the horrors he inflicted on those poor girls."

Hal gets up and pulls her close to him, his face inches from her own.

"You and your little friend stuck your fuckin' noses where they weren't wanted. Then you had the gall to come to my office and threaten me. *ME!* THE *MAYOR!*" Towering over her, hands in his pockets as he regards her on the old sofa—the powerful looking down on the weak, Caesar deciding the fate of a fighting slave. "I've done a lot over the years to get where I am now. It took a lot of time, a lot of effort. Compared to my own achievements, you are *nothing.*"

Ida looks up, fear washing away, calm rolling along in its place. "Being a racist like your friends?"

"If that's what I had to be associated with to get where I wanted to be, then so be it. Look, let me tell you something. I've never fully believed in the ideas of the KKK. But I learned a long time ago that they're ingrained in this town. They're old money—and that old money means everything when you're trying to control a whole town. So I used my association with them as a means to an end. For the greater good. And if a few blacks got hurt, or worse, well . . ."

Ida laughs. "Mr. Mayor, if you think keeping a group of people down serves the greater good, then you are definitely a racist."

"That's your opinion. You're not the first, and you won't be the last. When Daddy got diagnosed with dementia, I told him it was time I got incorporated into family affairs, with a deciding say. That meant running the company. Controlling the cash flow . . . and seeing that the old-timers got their tribute. They're some of the most powerful men in the country, Miss Lane, and they make a lot of money keeping Hope's Peak and the rest of the county just the way it is."

"Then I guess that's why they pushed you into the role of mayor, then," Ida says. "Protect their own interests."

"I won't deny that it helps to have these people on your side when running for office," Hal says, looking away, as if seeing something she doesn't. "And who knows what will come next—senator? Congressman? I have lofty ambitions, Miss Lane."

Ida strains against the tape around her wrists, but it's no good. She wonders what she would do if she got free.

Run?

Where to?

It's so dark outside, she'd probably break her neck in the process.

"Why're you telling me all this? I'm not stupid. I know you don't have any intentions of keeping me around."

Hal turns slowly. For a second, as the lamplight hits his teeth, she could swear they are sharp. A complete set of cannibal jaws. Looking at him, she sees it now. Sees the resemblance. Something in those cruel eyes of his. Hal squats down in front of her, smiling the whole time, the grin of a crazy person, a loony. Someone who has a serial killer's genes—who can perform unthinkable acts upon the living and not even blink.

"If your gift is real—as you say it is—then I want to know. I *need* to know what you saw when you touched my brother. It's been on my mind. We share the same DNA, he and I. And I wonder if we share a lot more."

She looks away—anything to break his hideous gaze—and the lightning explodes again outside, throwing everything in the house into stark relief. There, in the doorway, is Lester. Nothing but darkness where his eyes should be, his breath sucking the material of the hood in and out, in and out, and his chest heaving, covered in dried blood splatter. The head of the axe is soaked in blood, and she knows that it is Stu's.

Ida thinks of her grandparents' house, of the way the past seems to have seeped into the plaster on the walls, into the wooden beams. Into the floorboards, lodging its way into the grain. Getting absorbed by a structure, the old timbers sucking it up like a sponge. Haunted houses aren't inhabited by ghosts. They're a vessel for them. People are, too, especially when they connect with the dead the way Ida does.

The light fades, but Lester is burned into her retina. She clamps her eyes shut and can still see him looking back at her.

A hand covers her own. Ida opens her eyes. Watches as Hal pulls the end off a syringe with his teeth, and she barely has time to register what he is doing as he plunges it into her arm, injecting her with a clear, glassy liquid.

He sneers at her. Relishing her distress. Leaning close, he whispers, "You *will* tell me."

30

Harper's heart sinks when she sees the overturned truck. She applies the parking brake and gets out, grimacing from the sting of the rain. Wind snatching her breath away. Weinberg approaches, dressed in full waterproofs. "Detective, you're gonna get soaked."

"Any sign of a body?" she shouts over the storm.

Please say they've found her and sent her to the hospital.

Weinberg shakes his head. "Sorry."

Harper walks to the edge of the road and looks down. There is a team of officers surveying the scene, taking pictures, documenting what they can before the rain washes it all away.

"I can't explain it," Weinberg says, next to her. "Are you thinking she was pulled from the wreckage?"

"It would explain the second set of shoe prints, wouldn't it?" Harper shouts, almost to herself, her mind racing. "If it were anyone genuine, we'd have them showing up at one of the emergency rooms by now."

Weinberg nods. "Or they would have called it in and waited here."

"Exactly."

"So . . . where is she?"

Harper doesn't answer. She knew when she got the call from Weinberg that it was bad news. Her gut told her, and that instinct was something Captain Morelli put so much stock in.

"What do we do, then? This rain's not helping us come up with anything useful," Weinberg tells her.

Harper looks at him. "I wish I could tell you," she says.

◆ ◆ ◆

The room spins in a carousel of blurred colors. Ida's eyes are heavy—as if weighted down.

Hal holds her face in his hands, examining her. "You think it's kicked in?"

"She's stoned alright," Martin says from the doorway. "You can see it."

"Damn, that stuff kicks in fast. Where'd you get it, anyhow?"

"Some little punk we rolled out of here a few months back. I kept his stash at my place. Thought it might come in handy one day."

Hal looks at him, one eyebrow cocked. "What did we give her?"

"Fuck knows!" Martin says, then bursts into laughter.

"This isn't funny, Marty," Hal tells him, a definite growl in his voice. "I don't want her to OD before I know everything. I want the full picture here, d'you understand? The full fucking picture!"

"Alright, Hal. Jesus . . ."

"I'm not laughing, Marty. Be more careful next time. Let's get her off that sofa."

"Sure thing." Martin fetches a chair.

Ida looks at Hal. He has an aura around him. White fire. The smoke stinging her eyes is piling up off Hal's body, as if he is combusting. A man on fire.

"You're going to kill me," she says, her words slurred. Voice like honey, sticking to her tongue.

"Depends. If you tell me what I want to know . . . I might let you go," Hal tells her unconvincingly.

Ida smiles, shakes her head.

"Come on, we both know that's bullshit," she says sleepily. "You privileged white boys are all the same."

"We'll see," Hal says.

Martin returns with another chair. The two men lift her under the armpits and set her down on it. Ida closes her eyes, tries to drift away. Martin slaps the side of her face.

Hal sits opposite. "Look at me."

Ida tries—really tries. Her eyes won't focus. All she wants to do is sleep, but there's an electric current of resilience inside her that grief, incarceration, and loneliness have failed to weaken. Ida holds his gaze, despite wanting to give up. She does what she has always done.

Fights.

"LOOK AT ME," Hal demands, smoke billowing from his nostrils, his mouth, his ears.

"Trust me," Ida says, her eyeballs bulging. "I'm seein' you . . ."

Hal sits forward, his face mere inches away.

"I want to know everything," he growls. "Start at the beginning. The first victim . . . your mama."

Ida just looks at him.

"She was the template for every other murder after that. I should know. I covered 'em up," Hal admits, looking away. "Those girls of his with crowns on their heads. Everything started with Ruby Lane."

Ida runs her tongue over her dry, sore lips. She nods slowly. Hal reaches out for her hands, takes them in his own.

It happens.

Ida is tearing down a tunnel of light, of color. There is darkness at the end where the tunnel leads. Rushing into the darkness, her arms outspread, head tilted back, the black enveloping her in a dreadful cold blanket of ice that freezes every inch of her.

The connection has never been this instantaneous, this strong. This forceful. She is him, and he is her. She thinks: It's because he wants it, he has opened himself up to it.

A field, and Hal standing with a gun trained on a man. He is conflicted about what to do, his jealousy and his hurt causing him to pull the trigger. The shot cracks the veneer of the night, and Ida journeys through the fault line.

Then—a bed in a seedy motel room, the dim red light from outside cutting through the blinds in thick bars. A bathroom door opens, suddenly illuminating the scene, and a woman emerges, wiping her groin with a towel. "Came good that time, baby," she says to a man sitting on the edge of the bed, holding his head in his hands, as if ashamed.

When he looks up, Ida sees it is Hal as an impossibly young man. "This was a mistake."

The woman strokes the back of his neck. She's in her forties, face lined by stress and laughter, skin rough and coarse, tits succumbing to the pull of gravity.

"Well, if it's a mistake, it's an expensive one for you," she says. "Time to pay up, kid."

The room goes dark. Ida is free-falling through the night, to a field.

Now—Hal drives, his father pointing the way to an old house on the edge of town. When they get there, parked down the lane from it, Hal is able to recall riding past that house on his bike as a kid. When they spot Lester outside the house, hauling a bag of trash to the dumpster, Hal remembers him, too. He had more hair back then, and his shoulders weren't as stooped. But his face. How could you forget that face, with his lip all twisted up like that?

"That there is your brother," his father tells him, as if it is a fact of the world, like pollination or the movements of migratory species. "One of my dalliances from years ago. She was pretty back then, the mother. Wouldn't want to see her now, though. If she smiled, she'd crack your damned face."

Hal looks at him, not in disbelief but in anger. "Dalliances? How many affairs did you have?"

"That's not the issue here." His father lights a cigarette, snaps the lid of the Zippo shut with one flick of his wrist. "Christ, son, why d'you think you had no brothers or sisters? Once she had you, she all but dried up, barren as a cornfield in a summer drought. Weren't for lack of tryin' either, I can tell you. That woman had just one kid in her. It was inevitable I'd get one of my women on the side knocked up eventually."

Hal has to bite his bottom lip. Resist the urge to drag his old man out of the car and beat him with his bare hands. He wants to hurt something.

"Why are you telling me this?"

"Because your mother's gone. One day I'll be gone, too. Who's going to look out for your brother? Lester will be on his own."

"What's wrong with him?" Hal asks, watching Lester go back and forth.

"Deprived of oxygen? I don't know, son. What I do know is, he's my blood. I made him. He's a curse to me, for sure . . . but he's my curse. When I'm gone, I need you to do the right thing. Protect this family. Our legacy."

"You want me to step in," Hal says, shaking his head in disbelief.

His father looks at him, face bunching up with hate. His hand whips out, slapping the side of his son's face.

Hal doesn't react. Just takes the sting, the pain, as he always has.

"That out there is family. You do whatever it takes to protect your family, do you hear me?"

Hal nods slowly. It's not the first time his daddy has brought him in on a secret. But then, all of his secrets—the ones he's willing to share—are the kind of things he should be taking to the grave. Instead, they've formed a part of Hal's inheritance.

His father looks at him, intent. "Let me hear you say it."

Bitterly, Hal says, "Yes, Daddy."

Then—he stands among tall, dry grass, gazing down at a body on the ground. Ida sees a bare leg, the hem of a bloodstained dress high up on the *thighs. One hand, still clawed into the dusty earth. The last effort at clinging to this life, of fighting back the shadow of death.*

Sure enough—as if there were any doubt—a crown woven from supplejack vine sits atop the woman's head.

An older man walks through the grass to stand next to Hal. He smokes a cigar. "Awful."

"What are we gonna do about this?" Hal asks without looking at him.

The other detective—Lloyd Claymore—sucks on his cigar, not taking his eyes off the victim at their feet. Smoke trailing from his parted lips.

Hal shakes his head. Ida sees his eyes are red—this is not something he enjoys, not something he relishes. This is a burden, and it weighs on him. "I never asked for this."

"Me neither," the other man says. "But your daddy pays good money, and when you've seen one body, you've seen 'em all. This is for the good of the town . . . until we find this fucker."

Nobody knows of Hal's connection with these girls—his connection with the killer. The other cops that are involved in the cover-ups only know the damage it would do to Hope's Peak if the truth got out.

This is where the nickname started. With his comrades in arms. This is where they began to call him Honest Hal.

He squats down, lifts the girl's hand out of the dirt, holds her wrist. "So pretty."

The other man stands behind him. He spits on the ground. "I swear, if I ever catch this sick son of a bitch, I'm gonna make his death a long and painful one."

Hal glances over his shoulder. Still holding the dead girl's wrist. "Yeah."

Everything goes dark. Ida is pulled through the eternal night.

—Bodies.

There are a great many bodies on Hal's mind.

A lot of regret and sadness that he buries deep down inside, stuffing it away so that he can forget about it.

But if clothes maketh the man, so, too, do his mistakes.

Ida sees it—she feels it. Hal can try all he might to consume himself with his lust for power, with his eradication of anybody linking him to the dark deeds of the past. But there is no escape from his own conscience.

She felt no such remorse in Lester. But in Hal, it is a bubbling cauldron of emotion that he struggles to keep subdued.

Wisher's Pond. Snow on the ground. Ida cannot bear to look, but there are no eyes to close. There is no way of unseeing her mother lying there, like an angel, all frosted over. The men stood around her, Hal among them, not understanding what all this means, not knowing that his connection to Ruby Lane is immediate.

Ignorant of what is coming.

Hal telling his father that they need to have Lester locked away. Shouting at him, breaking down, telling him that he can't continue to cover for him anymore. His daddy slapping him in the face, once, twice, and berating him for being a traitor to his family. "He's my responsibility! One day, he'll be yours!"

The connection is breaking—Hal is removing his hands from hers, and any second the bond will be cut completely. Ida sees a woman sitting opposite Hal in a diner. She glances about, then slides a baby scan across the table.

He picks it up, frowning. "A baby?"

"I'm eighteen weeks," *she tells him.* "You're going to be a father."

He puts the scan down, stunned, then gets to his feet. "No . . . I'm not," *he says, stalking out.*

Now—Hal is a boy, his face pressed against a gap in the door to his parents' bedroom. His mother on the bed, where she has been the past few weeks. Dying, Hal has been told, from some kind of cancer. All he knows is that his mother has become a pale imitation of her former self. A skeleton that can't move, can't do anything but whimper and whine from the pain.

Hal's breath catches in his throat as he watches his father pushing a pillow down on his mother's face. His father crying, howling from what he feels compelled to do.

Suffocating her.

Killing her.

Ending the pain.

Hal wants to run. Wants to collapse on the floor, his legs turned to jelly. But he watches. He watches until the end, when his father slowly pulls the pillow away, observes the stillness that has set like ice in his wife's face. His daddy takes a step back from the bed, crosses himself over the chest. A silent prayer.

Hal backs up, light from the room throwing a bar through the gap in the door. He keeps stepping back until he is in darkness.

Then—a lamp. An old man sleeps in a bed, and Ida watches as a grown Hal takes a pillow and presses it down on the old man's face until he is still. Tears streaming down Hal's face, hanging like raindrops from his jowls. He pushes and pushes until his daddy's black fire has been extinguished. Until, when he lifts the pillow, there is his father's face, frozen in terror. Eyes bulging from the sockets, tongue clenched between the old man's yellowed teeth. Hal backs up, still holding the pillow in his hands. He can't tear his eyes away from his daddy's death face, but then he looks up, and he looks straight at Ida.

With that, the connection is broken.

Hal falls back, knocking his own chair over in his haste to get away from her. Forehead slick with sweat, the color has drained from his face to the extent that he's taken on a deathly pallor. Martin helps him to his feet.

"You okay, mate? Did you get what you wanted?" Martin asks.

Hal produces his cell with shaking hands.

"No. Get the tape. Put it across her eyes. Tape her mouth shut," he gasps, visibly shaken. "I don't want her looking at me. I don't want her making a sound."

"What did she do to you?" Martin asks.

"Just fucking do it!" Hal yells at him.

Ida's head swims from the drugs and the residual connection. Her heart slogs its labored rhythm in her chest.

As Hal dials a number and holds the phone to his ear, Martin closes in on Ida with the duct tape.

Everything goes dark.

31

Harper huddles in her car to answer her cell, dripping wet from being outside. "Albie?"

"Hey."

"I, uh, thought you weren't talking to me."

Albie sighs. "I'm sorry for acting that way, boss. What can I say? I was a bit . . . upset."

"No need to apologize. I got you into that mess."

"Well, look, Freehan let me come back. Had to beg her, mind you," Albie says.

"She revoked the suspension?"

"Yeah. I think she realized she needs every hand available for this investigation."

Harper exhales heavily. "And yet she keeps me suspended . . ."

"Look, I heard about Ida's truck. I've got a potential lead," he tells her. "It could end up as nothing, for all I know. But it's worth a shot."

"At this point, I'm willing to try anything. We've just got to find her."

"We will," Albie assures her. "There was a Volvo seen heading in the same direction as Ida. A traffic cam picked it up early on; it looks like it may have been following her. I mean, it's a long shot, but it would fit with the report the response team issued, about the vehicle that ran her off the road being built like a tank. I mean, that truck is a heavy old motherfucker."

"That's all well and good, Albie, but it's a bit of a stretch," Harper says, thinking to herself: *Even so, I'll clutch at any straw if it means I can get her back alive.* The phone vibrates in her hand. She holds it in front of her. "I've got another caller. Let me call you back," she says, ending the current conversation and answering the incoming call.

"Detective Harper? Is this you?"

"Yes," she says. "Who is this?"

"You know who," the voice says, and she instantly knows. "I have something of yours . . . or, shall I say, some*one*."

Harper's heart sinks. "Ida."

"Yes."

"How did you get my number?"

A chuckle. "I have my ways."

"What do you want?"

"I want you to present yourself to me. Right here."

The sound of his breathing on the other end of the line. Voice stripped back to how he really sounds, minus the Honest Hal veneer. A privileged, lisp-free version of his murderous brother.

"Where is *here*?"

A dry chuckle. "Where it all began, Detective, of course."

Despite everything she feels, every new instinct blossoming inside her as she nears parenthood, Harper hears herself saying: "Don't hurt her. I'll give myself to you if you let her go. She's been through enough."

And at the same time, she knows there is more to think about than herself. More to think about than Ida. There is an unborn child.

"Come alone. Tell nobody about this. Give yourself to me. Do that, and we've got a deal, Detective. Don't . . . and she dies."

The line goes dead. Harper stares at the phone in her hand, her mind racing. She considers the direction the Volvo was traveling. The mayor telling her, *"Where it all began."*

Everything goes back to one person: Lester Simmons.

Where did all of this start?

Lester's childhood.

Lester's mother.

Lester's *house.*

Harper thinks of Ida there in that place, and what that must be like for her to endure. It takes all her willpower to turn the key in the ignition, slip the car into gear, and head off.

Weinberg staring at her in confusion from the roadside.

Back toward Hope's Peak, the night illuminated by green, red, and yellow lights. Harper's hand pats the holster on her hip. Then it moves to her stomach.

This isn't San Francisco. I'm not putting work first. I'm following my heart, which is the only thing I know to do.

Her phone lights up, vibrating on the passenger seat. She glances across at it and sees the name of the caller: ALBIE. Calling her back after she cut him off.

Harper doesn't answer it. *He's been involved enough, and this is my mess to deal with. I have to settle this score . . . alone.*

The streetlamps on Main Street sway back and forth in the wind. The late-night café is about the only place still open—the rest have had the sense to close shop. Tie everything down until the storm passes. Rainwater gurgles in the gutters. A loose shutter bangs in the wind. The two detectives dive inside their car, slamming the doors behind them.

"I was enjoying my coffee," Ramirez says, irritated. "You better be sure about this."

"Sorry. I couldn't just sit in there," Albie says, clipping his seat belt in. "She's going to go there alone, I know it."

"Where?"

"The Simmons house."

Ramirez shakes his head. "Slow down a second. You've lost me."

"Ida was run off the road. Pulled out of her truck. The only vehicle heading out that way that was big enough to have rammed her truck was also traveling in the direction of the Simmons place."

"You're takin' some pretty big leaps there," Ramirez says. "But the reasoning is sound. Why kidnap this woman in the first place? And what's the significance of taking her there?"

Albie starts the engine. "We believe the mayor is Lester Simmons's brother. Or something like that. He's related. Covering up for him all these years. We don't understand everything about it yet, so I know it sounds crazy."

"No shit," Ramirez says, chewing it over. "Okay. I guess that old house would be the last place anyone would look for her."

"Precisely."

Ramirez frowns. "And this Ida . . . she's the one who's meant to be a psychic, am I right?"

"Yeah. Lester killed her mom."

Ramirez clips himself in. "Well, we better get going."

"You don't have to do this."

"Yes, I do."

"I appreciate it."

"Cut the shit, kid," Ramirez says, checking his sidearm for ammo. "Drive."

◆ ◆ ◆

Martin returns from the side of the house—the only way in and out because of the metal shutters over every door and window. "She just got here."

Hal examines his pistol, checks that it has ammunition, weighs it in his hands. It's been a while since he held the gun, let alone fired it. But it's like riding a bicycle; you never forget what it feels like. "Get out there, Marty. I want her unarmed."

Martin removes his own gun, a small stubby that Hal knows packs a punch despite its size. No silencer needed this time. With the storm bearing down on Hope's Peak, neighboring houses won't be aware of any gunshots.

"Got it," Martin says, walking off.

"Hey," Hal says.

Martin turns around.

"I really appreciate your dedication, Marty. It won't go unrewarded."

"Honored, mate," he says, leaving the house, becoming one with the dark.

Hal stands in the doorway to the living room, gun at his side, watching the kitchen for a sign of anyone walking through. The drugs have knocked Ida out. Her chin rests on her chest, and there is a trail of drool down one side of her mouth.

She saw into me as much as I saw into her.

He flexes his hand on the handle of the gun, eyes narrowed as he remembers what he experienced. What he saw. *Touching her mother and passing out from the connection that was made. Meeting Jane Harper and helping with the investigation. Pressing her hands on Lester as he died, experiencing his free fall into darkness.*

Hal blinks, thinking: *Is that all there is? Is that what we've got to look forward to when the end comes?*

He can remember believing that Lester was done with his obsession. That he'd stop killing for good. There were no dead girls for a long time, and he thought—naively—that his brother had gotten it out of his system. So he cut ties with everyone who'd helped him blow smoke over the facts. Focused on himself. On his mayoral campaign.

He relaxed and dedicated himself to the work at hand. Fulfilling the will of the elders that he win the election.

Then a dead girl was discovered. A crown on her head. Lester's handiwork—and Hal wasn't there to stop it from being discovered. Wasn't there to protect the interests of the town. Reeling from it, unsure what he should do, Hal panicked. He went to the elders and admitted that he didn't know how to contain it. Didn't know how to continue protecting the town with a murderer on the loose. He made assurances that there wouldn't be any more victims.

Then another girl turned up.

Hal had lived in fear that what connected him to Lester would be discovered any day. But when that discovery wasn't made and Lester was killed, he considered himself out of the red. He visited his brother in the morgue to pay his final respects. There were similarities. Little things. Lester looked a lot like their father, when he'd been near to the end. Before Hal had suffocated the old man with a pillow and finished him for good.

With Lester out of the way, there would be no more bodies. No more young women getting found in empty fields—no more leavings of a sick, deranged mind. Lester was a magpie, and the girls were fragile shiny things he coveted with a simple, dark desire.

But then the allegations came. Harper's report detailing the cover-up, stirring everything up. He wasn't worried about Internal Affairs—the head of IA was an elder. He'd make sure that Hal wasn't implicated in the conspiracy, but only because Hal had assured him that his former foot soldiers were loyal detectives who'd all taken bribes and had their own reputations to protect. Morelli was the only problem there. He'd been clean in the old days, didn't understand the larger needs of the town that were incumbent upon the police captain to protect. Still, he could be dealt with. Then word had come that Bill Marshall was getting cold feet, had made an appointment to talk to IA. The elders wanted action. They couldn't have their future in Hope's Peak put at risk because somebody might reveal the genetic link between the mayor and a prolific serial killer. So Hal took things into his own hands . . . the way Daddy would have wanted it. The way he watched him take Roofy, when he was a kid, and shove him into the back of his car.

He took ownership of the problem and sought to provide his own solution . . .

◆　◆　◆

Harper gets out of the car and looks up at the house. A shiver runs through her entire body at the sight of it.

Night sky a tempest of roiling dark clouds, the house stands blacker than black against the backdrop of the storm, as if a silhouette of something that doesn't truly exist. Rain cuts in from the side at an angle.

Sharp as nails.

Harper unholsters her sidearm. Holding it low, she starts up toward the house. A lone figure stands at the side of the building, watching her. She raises her pistol and aims it at him.

"Freeze! Don't move!"

The man doesn't budge an inch. "If you want to save your friend, leave your weapon on the ground."

Harper keeps her gun trained on him, not knowing what to do. She hears an approaching vehicle. Turns to face it. Lights from the car spill out over the road, illuminating her on one side. Harper shields her eyes. Looks back up at the house.

The man is gone.

Harper hurries to the side of the car as Albie and Ramirez get out. "Christ, what're you two doing here?"

"We're your backup," Albie says, expecting her to be pleased.

Thunder breaks behind the house, filling the sky with electric fire.

Harper shoves Albie. "You idiot, you're going to get yourself killed!"

"Harper?"

"Damn it!" She glances back at the house. "I didn't want anyone else involved . . ."

Ramirez yanks his sidearm free from his holster. "Are we rocking and rollin' or not?"

"Ramirez, you're nearly retired."

"Your point?"

A gunshot issues from the side of the house, then another. The windshield of Albie's car implodes.

"Down!" Harper yells as she throws herself behind the car.

Another shot, this one whizzing through the air.

"Are you wearing a vest?" Albie hisses.

Harper shakes her head. "No. I take it you're not either."

The rain is in her eyes, making it hard to see. Ramirez moves, crouched low, ducking down behind a bush at the front of the property. He leans up, fires in the direction of their shooter, aiming blind. His shots are thrown wide by the wind, most of them hitting the house. Smashing into the metal shutters, ricocheting away.

Harper cups her hands around her mouth to amplify her voice. "You're outgunned! Show yourself!"

It's silent except for the mayhem of the storm itself. Harper considers following Ramirez's lead, but she knows it will only expose them both. Albie darts out around the car and makes a dash for the dilapidated front gate at the edge of the property. It hangs to one side of the post, rotten and peeling. Albie jumps over it, runs up the front path. The man by the house fires again. Albie flinches, dives behind a fallen trash can for cover, hitting the soaking-wet grass.

Harper sees the flash from up near the porch. Moves, keeping low. Ramirez follows her lead. They charge the house, firing their weapons, breaking either side to confuse their target. Albie pops up from behind the trash can, centering on his target, unloading his weapon.

There is a sudden, surprised, "Oomph!"

Ramirez stands off to one side, and the two of them watch as a man staggers out from the shadows, clutching his stomach. There is no gun to be seen.

"Stop! Stay where you are, you son of a bitch!" Harper yells, closing in on him with her gun in front of her. Lightning crashes overhead, filling the sky with sickly light. The man's eyes are misted over. Blood seeps out of the wound, oozing like cherry jam between his fingers.

Ramirez presses in on him. "Down on the ground!"

Harper waves her hand. "Ramirez, wait!"

The older detective doesn't hear her. "I said down on the ground!"

The man just looks at him. Stumbles forward. Ramirez fires. The man's head flies back as if struck by a great weight. He drops to the ground, a gaping hole in his face.

"Ramirez!"

Instead of holstering his weapon, he turns it on her.

She freezes, unsure what is happening. "Hey . . ."

"Drop your piece."

Harper doesn't know what to do.

"DO IT!" he screams, stamping forward. His finger itching to pull the trigger—to apply the pressure necessary to end her life.

Harper tosses her gun onto the grass. "There. I've done it."

Albie can't hear them over the wind. He watches Harper throw her piece.

"What's going on up there?"

Ramirez turns, points his gun at Albie, and fires.

"NO!" Harper screams, flying forward.

Ramirez catches her by the throat with one hand, driving her back, the rain hammering them both, roaring thunder and lightning smashing the sky wide open. Ramirez shoves her back onto the slimy wet grass. He unhooks the handcuffs off his belt. "Put these on."

"You've got to let me help him . . ."

Ramirez shakes his head. "Albert's gone, Jane. Shot in the line of duty. There's no helping him now."

Harper keeps her eyes on him, but picks the cuffs up. "Why do this, Ramirez? Whatever's going on, you and I can figure a way out."

He snorts. "And here I was thinkin' you were hot shit. But you'll see. This job takes everything from you, and when you try to claw just a little for yourself, something comes along and claims it back. Leaves you with nothin'. I hear you were married before you came out here. I had two ex-wives by the time I was your age. My pension was spent before I even came close to retirement age. Why else do you think I'm still here? I earned what I got tucked away by following my superiors' orders. Protecting this town from the truths that would only hurt it. And now I should just sit back until IA gets around to dragging my name through the mud like they were about to do with Bill Marshall's? Not happening."

Harper snaps the cuffs on her wrists, binding them together. She fights the urge to run to Albie, disregard the prospect of Ramirez shooting her in the back, just to see if he is alive. But Harper holds herself in check, swallows the impulse down, contains it, takes a steadying breath. "We have to call an ambulance."

"That's not happening. Get up." Ramirez grabs the top of her arm and shoves her forward, past the fallen body of Hal Crenna's henchman. Harper can't help but look at his face—or what is left of it. "Inside."

She continues around the side of the house, Ramirez at her back. Not in a million years did she ever imagine that she'd have cause to return here.

To this house, where Stu lost his life.

It's dark, and she can't see where she is going. She's at gunpoint, almost certainly about to get killed. All she can think of is Albie, back there on the wet ground. She can't help but hate herself for putting him in harm's way.

I should have called for backup. Last time someone made a mistake like this, he got himself killed because he was alone and couldn't anticipate what was coming. Now here I am, repeating that awful mistake. On my own, walking toward certain death, with so much undone. Only this time, I've got others killed, too.

Harper hesitates at the threshold of an open door, the house exhaling its cold, stinking breath in her face. Damp. Mildew. Decay. Ramirez gives her a shove, and she staggers forward, blindly, into the dark.

The belly of the beast.

32

The hall looks the same—broken wood over the staircase from when she fell with Lester. Harper looks at the dirty floor, at the spot where Stu died. There's no blood, but she can still see it. On the opposite side of the hall, Harper remembers calling to Ida to throw her her gun. Lifting it. Aiming it at Lester. Firing. The force of the shot throwing the monster back.

The air is tainted by the stench of fuel. Harper looks around but can't see any sign of spilled gasoline.

"That you, Marty?" a voice calls through from the room adjoining the hall.

"It's Ramirez," he says, edging her forward.

Hal Crenna appears in the doorway. His eyes drift down to the cuffs on her wrists, gleaming in the dim light inside the house. Hal smiles at the sight of her.

"Just like you asked," Ramirez says.

Hal looks up. "And Marty?"

"Gone," Ramirez tells him, holstering his piece.

Hal sighs. "Regrettable, but he was fast becoming a liability."

"Yeah." Ramirez nods. "I know what you mean."

"Do you?" Hal asks, lifting his pistol. Without another word, he fires, shooting the old detective in the chest. Ramirez is thrown back, smashes into the wall, and lands clutching his chest with his hands. Hot dark blood floods out, spurting down his torso. He looks up from his hands with terrified eyes—disbelieving that the tables have turned on him.

His mouth makes a weird sucking sound as he tries to speak. *"Fpuh! Fpuh! Fpuh!"*

Hal aims. Fires again. And again.

The house is filled with the stench of powder and smoke. Harper's ears ring as she flinches from the gunshots. Ramirez tenses, face contorted with pain, then collapses in a heap, head down, arms loose at his sides.

"This way. Unless you want to join him."

Harper walks into the room, relieved to see Ida.

The mayor directs Harper to the sofa. "Sit."

She does as she's told. "Will she be alright? What have you given her?" Harper asks.

Hal smiles. "None of this will matter soon."

"How come?"

"Why d'you think?" Hal sneers at her. He walks to a gasoline canister in the far corner. "I've been busy preparing for your cremation. Before this storm is over, I'll be back home with a good glass of scotch. You'll all be here. All of my problems taken care of in one place."

"You're going to burn the house down."

"With you in it. Of course, nobody will know I was ever here," Hal says, looking up. "A bonfire of freedom, you could say. Setting fire to my past for good. But first, I want you to know why I've done this. I want you to know how it feels to have someone you care for taken away from you."

"How could you feel anything for someone like that?"

"He was my brother. Blood is blood," he says with a resigned shrug. He aims the gun at Ida's head. She is unconscious, her mouth and eyes taped, nostrils flaring with slow, steady breathing.

"We had a deal. You said you wouldn't hurt her," Harper says.

"It's inevitable, Detective."

"Please, you must know what she's been through. By your brother's hand, no less," Harper says.

She spots movement out in the hall. Something shifting in the shadows. Drawing closer. In her heart of hearts, she hopes it is what she thinks it is. Backup.

"You don't know the pressures of being *me*," Hal says, readying himself to pull the trigger.

The movement in the hall takes shape, becomes the wounded form of Albie staggering into the living room, gun in hand. The weak light of the gas lamp on the table reaches him, and his weary eyes connect with Harper's.

Hal frowns, turns his head to face the doorway as Albie presents himself. Hal spins about, lifts his weapon. Harper leaps from the sofa. Hooks her cuffed wrists under his chin and pulls back, hard. Hal falls back against her, discharging his gun into the ceiling, sending a cloud of rotten plaster showering down from above.

"Get his weapon!"

Albie grabs Hal's gun hand, wrestling it from him as Harper does her best to strangle him from behind. The mayor of Hope's Peak is stronger than either of them is counting on, driving his elbow into Harper's midsection, winding her.

He gets up, surges forward like a bull, heading for Albie. The wounded detective shifts to one side, enough for Hal to go barreling past, hitting the table. He careens off to the side and falls against the gas canister, knocking it over.

Its contents spill out beneath him. Hal looks at his hands, dripping wet with fuel.

Albie heads for the door. Harper tries to rouse Ida, but she is out cold, so she pulls her from the chair, drags her through the door to the hall. Hal pulls himself up against the table. His weight upends it, the gas lamp tumbling to the floor, smashing open.

The fuel ignites. Flames burst out across the floor, up Hal's legs, catching on his clothes. The mayor rises screaming from the table, his whole body on fire. He stumbles out after them, his voice a thin, reedy screech as the inferno consumes him.

Harper rushes out of his way. Albie helps her to pull Ida clear.

Hal falls to his knees in the hall, screaming in agony. He falls forward, writhing, collapsing on the very spot where his brother, Lester, met his maker.

Between them, they drag Ida outside into the storm. They fall back on the muddy ground as the fire that began in the living room ignites the gas Hal doused the rest of the house with. It consumes the place from the inside, swiftly becoming a blazing furnace that the falling rain is unable to contain.

Harper fumbles her phone from her pocket and dials 911 as Albie passes out next to her.

"No, no, no, don't die on me now."

She clamps her hand down on the bullet wound to his chest, applying as much pressure as she can, watching the firelight fill the night sky.

Through the open door, there is only fire.

As she looks about, one hand against Albie's chest, the other holding her phone to her ear, Harper thinks that she sees something moving in there. A lone figure among the flames. She squints, watching as it becomes a man. There is a white hood on his head. An axe in his hand.

Lester.

She can't look away. The house is burning down, timbers popping, walls and ceilings crashing down inside. Though they're dangerously close to it, Harper can't move. A voice speaks in her ear, but she doesn't hear it. Lester is looking down at something on the floor, head bowed.

Hal.

The flames rise. Harper blinks, stares into the fire, but *he* is gone . . . if he'd ever truly been there in the first place. Hell rages inside the house, consuming everything.

33

Two Days Later

"Place looks the best it ever has," Ida says.

The Simmons house burned to the ground in the fire, and despite the rainwater that fell on it that night, it smolders still. Damp gray smoke rising into the pale sky.

"I'm inclined to agree with you," Harper says. The storm reached its peak that night, dissipating the morning after—leaving in its wake littered streets, burst drains, broken windows, damaged rooftops . . . and one dead mayor.

Ida rubs Harper's back. "How're you feeling, sugar?"

"Okay," Harper says, looking at the house from the roadside. "All things considered."

Ida says, "A pregnant woman getting shot at so many times in one week . . . it's gotta be a record."

Harper stands taller. "I don't *look* pregnant, though . . . Do I?"

"Well, it's getting there."

Harper's shoulders sag. "I don't know how this is ever going to work, Ida. Doing this job, it's like you can't have anything else. Ramirez said something similar."

"Ramirez turned out to be a bad man," Ida says.

"Yes, but he had a point. I don't know if I'll ever be able to balance both a job and a family."

"You will. I'll be here to help."

Harper smiles. "Oh look. Here you are fussing over me when *you're* the one who was drugged up to your eyeballs."

Ida still looks peaky. Frail and weak. She should have stayed in the hospital at least another day, but she discharged herself that morning. "Oh, you know me," she says. "I'll get through it."

"Ida . . ."

"Sugar, I'm just glad to be alive."

Harper thinks: *Finally, it's finished.*

A car approaches, and the two of them watch as it comes to a halt. Captain Freehan climbs out from the back seat, walks up to them looking tired but resilient. At first Harper didn't like the woman. In fact, she doubted her motives. But thrust into the same situation, she doubts she would have acted differently.

Damage control first and foremost. And in that regard, Harper *was* the damage.

"Thought I'd find you both here," Freehan says, looking at the charred, skeletal remains of the Simmons house.

Ida sighs. "Doesn't feel real."

"It will," Freehan assures her. "In time. You'll realize it's all behind you."

"How's Albie?" Harper asks.

"Out of it," Freehan says. "How that boy made it into the house is beyond me. A shot to the chest like that . . . he should be dead."

Harper smiles. "He's made of tough stuff."

"Certainly is."

"Is his partner, Jon, with him?"

"Right next to him, holding his hand the entire time."

"What's the prognosis?"

"They're optimistic. The bullet missed a major artery. He just needs to mend," Freehan tells her, breaking into a smile. "Few weeks off work, he'll be right as rain. I expect Albert back at work and reporting for duty right away."

Harper can't help but grin. "Damn right."

Freehan shakes her head. "I'm joking, of course. He can take as long as he wants. Same for you. Don't worry about pay; I'll square it. Least I can do."

"Thank you."

Freehan starts to leave, but turns back at the last moment. "By the way, I had that glass tested."

Harper's eyebrows peak with surprise. "Yes?"

Freehan turns to Ida. "You had a rough time of things. I'm very sorry about that. Seems you were right. They were half brothers. Maybe if you'd said something sooner . . ."

"Would you have believed me if I had?" Ida asks.

"Probably not."

"I figured as much," Ida says.

"How are you feeling, anyway? That was quite a cocktail you were injected with," Freehan says.

"I'm doin' okay. I feel stronger than I did. I guess I'm getting whatever it was he injected me with out of my system."

"Maybe you should have stayed in the hospital," Harper chides her.

Ida rolls her eyes. "I'll be just fine."

"You know, you're a good cop, Harper," Freehan says, smiling softly. "A little impulsive, perhaps, but you follow your nose. Even if that means poking it in places it shouldn't be."

Harper is unsure what to say.

"And by the looks of things, I was wrong to make assumptions about Morelli."

"Who could blame you?"

"He was tainted by the knowledge that officers under his watch were corrupt, but he had no part in any of the cover-ups, of that I am sure."

Harper cocks an eyebrow. "And Internal Affairs?"

"They seem to be of the same opinion. I'll see to it his record is untainted. I guess this town owes the man that much." Freehan looks at the burnt house. "This case is going to blow up in a big way. There will be a lot of questions. A lot of inquiries. A serial killer, a cover-up spanning decades, the murder of the captain of police, the mayor of the town assassinating key witnesses to the case . . . I mean, I've sure inherited a helluva mess here."

"Do you think you can pull the department through it?" Harper asks.

Freehan walks to the car, opens the door, and turns back. "I believe I can. It'll be painful, but we'll get there. There is something I need to do first, though . . . and I've been meaning to do it since I arrived."

Harper looks at Ida and then back to Freehan, frowning. "And what's that?"

"Have a drink."

◆ ◆ ◆

As they drive through town, Ida looks out the window. "I'll be living close by soon. I said yes to an apartment."

"Oh. You didn't say."

"I was coming back from the leasing agent when I was . . . well, you know . . ."

"Oh," Harper says. "Right."

They stop at a set of lights. Trash is strewn across the streets. Several store windows were smashed by flying debris during the storm. The town has never looked so run-down. But maybe it needed to hit rock bottom before it could rise up again. She'd like to believe that Crenna's death means the end of the evil that has been poisoning the town for decades, but unsaid by all of them is that Crenna, power hungry as he was, couldn't have orchestrated everything alone. There are still others out there who enabled him, enabled Lester Simmons. Maybe even controlled the town from behind the scenes. Hopefully, in time, the ongoing Internal Affairs investigation will see to them . . .

Ida shifts in her seat. "So, uh, do I get to tell you now? I feel like I owe you. I mean, you *did* save my life."

"You know it's not like that," Harper says, rolling her eyes. "There isn't a score to keep, Ida. Besides, I endangered your life by getting you involved in all of this to begin with."

Ida shakes her head. "No way. I have this gift. It's about time I used it for somethin'. Used it for good. I'll never run from my abilities again."

Harper thinks: *And I'll stop running from the past.*

Ida says, "Just let me tell you, okay? A little gift?"

Harper sighs. "Go on, then. But I'm not happy about it."

"Really? Even if I tell you that you're having a girl?"

Harper grins. "A girl? You're sure?"

"Sugar," Ida says, laughing. "That baby is you all over. Trust me. A miniature Jane Harper, for sure. Just waiting to come out and start taking names."

Harper's hand goes to her stomach. The part of her that has always appreciated the life of a cop, the freedom of moving to Hope's Peak and not having to answer to anyone, the part of her that has enjoyed being the lone wolf . . . all of that feels diminished by the thought of the life growing inside her. *Did I ever think it was possible to care for and love something the way I love this baby? Even if it doesn't feel real?*

Harper knows the answer to that. Deep down, she's always known it.

"You know, I think everything is going to be alright," Harper says, looking at Ida.

"Me, too, sugar," Ida says. "Me, too."

EPILOGUE

Dawn breaks over Hope's Peak, cutting through the blue haze. In the cemetery overlooking the town, a lone woman climbs the hill and lays a bouquet of flowers on a grave before sitting on the cool grass next to it. As the sun rises, she fills the occupant of the grave in on what he has missed.

The woman tells him that they are expecting a baby girl and that she will do her damnedest to see that their daughter has a good life—the *best* life.

She unwraps a lemon sherbet as she talks. By the time she has finished speaking, the sky is fresh and filled with warmth. A new day has begun—filled with possibilities.

ACKNOWLEDGMENTS

The author would like to thank the following people for their assistance and support with this book:

Bernard Schaffer, who gave me the kind of tough love I needed to hear; David K. Hulegaard for his honest feedback on an earlier draft of the book; my "Constant Reader" and Irish warrior, Barbara Spencer; the authors I have connected with since joining Thomas & Mercer—Jay Stringer, Mark Edwards, Joe Hart, Susan McBride, and so many others; my agent, Sharon Pelletier at Dystel, Goderich & Bourret, for being a constant source of support and encouragement; Jacquelyn Ben-Zekry, who showed me ways to make Hal Crenna live and breathe as a villain; Caitlin Alexander, editor, to whom I owe a debt of gratitude; the author and screenwriter Blake Crouch, who gave me a crash course in selling a book in fifteen seconds; Jessica Tribble, Gracie Doyle, and Sarah Shaw at Thomas & Mercer; and of course a huge thank-you to my wife, Lesley—without your support I wouldn't have the time, or space, to do what I do. You remain, as always, my rock.

I've said this before, and I'll keep saying it: the biggest thanks goes to you, dear reader. Having you read these pages means the world.

—TH

About the Author

Photo © 2016 Lesley Healey

Tony Healey is the bestselling author of the Far From Home series and *Hope's Peak*, the first book in his Harper and Lane series. His fiction has appeared alongside such award-winning authors as Alan Dean Foster and Harlan Ellison. He lives with his wife and four daughters in Sussex, England, and is at work on his next novel.